# THE CHOSEN WITCH

## THE COVEN: ELEMENTAL MAGIC PREQUEL NOVELLA

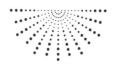

## CHANDELLE LAVAUN

WANDERLOST PUBLISHING

# PROLOGUE

Every time I looked back, the darkness swallowed me. The shadows moved, like they were trying to reach out and grab me. All I heard were footsteps and branches breaking. Daddy said he'd follow us, except it sounded too big to be him.

I reached out for my mother's hands and called to her, "Momma, wait for me!"

She slid her fingers through mine and squeezed real hard. "I'm right here, baby."

Momma held my hand tight the whole time we ran through the bushes. I wanted her to carry me, but she had to hold my little sister instead. When we stopped at the edge of the water, she let go of my hand and crouched down. I reached out and gripped the sleeve of her soft white dress, not wanting her to get too far away. Her dress was wet and sticky, but I held on anyway. "Momma, can we stop running now?"

"I'm sorry, baby, no. We don't have much time." She held her palm out, closed her eyes, and began humming. Her yellow hair flew all around her and brushed over my face.

A light flashed. When I looked down, a small wooden boat sat in the dirt at Momma's bare feet. This didn't scare me though. I was used to Momma and Daddy creating things that weren't there before.

Momma raised my sister's little sleeping face to her own and kissed her forehead. She gasped and held Hope's face to hers. Momma's eyes squeezed shut real tight, but her tears slipped out anyway. Her whole body shook, so I held on tighter so she wouldn't fall over.

She hugged Hope close and whispered against her cheek, "I love you more than a thousand stars, Hope. Please forgive me. May the Goddess bless you."

My heart burned and sounded like thunder in my ears. I stepped close and put my hand on Momma's shoulder, blinking away my tears. "Momma?" I said, but my voice cracked.

She carefully placed Hope down into the little boat. A second later, a blanket that hadn't been there before was tucked around Hope, snuggling her in like her bed at home. Momma mumbled under her breath, but no matter how hard I concentrated, I couldn't understand them. She reached into her satchel, pulled out flower petals and small crystals, and placed them into the boat, covering Hope's body.

I gripped her dress a little tighter. Where was my boat? I wanted to go with my sister. How could we follow her if we didn't have boats too? "Momma, where is Hope going? Are we going too?"

She didn't answer me. Her eyes were full of tears and her lips trembled. She reached up behind her neck and pulled off her favorite locket. The one she never, ever took off. My heart pounded in my chest even harder. I tried to speak, but nothing came out. My throat was tight, like there was something stuck in it. Momma leaned forward and wrapped the necklace around Hope's neck. Her fingers shook as she tucked the locket under the blankets.

"Stay here, love." Momma said to me before carrying the raft into the river.

"Momma?" I shouted. "Momma!"

With one hand on the raft and the other raised up to the moon, she called out to the Goddess and prayed. After a few seconds, she pushed the raft into the water...and let go.

"NO! Hope!" I screamed and ran into the river.

The ice cold water splashed all the way up to my knees. Momma caught me and wrapped her arms around my body, holding me in place while I screamed.

My nose burned, and tears filled my eyes so much I

couldn't see. I opened my mouth and strained to breathe. I cried and wiggled, trying to get free to catch my sister. "Momma! Hope! Get her, get her! Hurry!"

Momma picked me up and carried me back to the dirt. She dropped to her knees so my feet touched and our green eyes were at the same level. Hers were full of tears and kept spilling onto her cheeks like rivers. She slid her hands down to squeeze my fingers. Her hands were warm and soft. "Baby, look at me."

"Momma, I don't understand."

"I know, baby." She smiled but it looked a little wobbly since her lips were shaking. "You are so strong, so brave. Hope is not lost. You will find her again one day."

She reached up and pulled off her other favorite necklace, an old key on a leather cord, and looped it over my head. I gasped and stepped back to look at it. The gold metal looked almost black without lights, and it stung like ice against my stomach, even through my shirt.

Momma cleared her throat. "One day you will find her, and this key will help. Until then, the Goddess will keep her safe. Where they can't find her."

"Who? Who's gonna find her, Momma? Where's Daddy?" I had so many questions. I wanted to talk about Hope and Daddy more.

My head was light and fuzzy. Thunder rumbled over my head, and the sky lit up the brightest white I'd ever seen. The ground shook under my feet. I cried out and grabbed onto Momma's dress. She pulled me up and squeezed me so tight I could barely breathe. Her fingers dug into my skin.

Water filled my eyes, and I tried to blink it away but it wouldn't stop. "Momma? I'm scared."

"Oh, baby." She sat me back down and cupped my face in her warm, soft hands. "Don't be. You are so strong. The Goddess will protect you. It's time we say goodbye now."

I gasped. "Goodbye? No! I don't want to leave you."

"But you must. My time here is done. Before sunrise I will be with your father." Her eyebrows scrunched down and her face twisted. She turned away and cried.

Tears poured down my face. Now my lips were shaking too. "But then I'll be alone."

She wiped her wet face on her sleeve before turning to look at me. "No, baby. You will never be alone. You must run now and not look back. The Tennessee wilds will protect you. Run through there until you get to Eden. The Goddess will send you guidance."

"No, Momma, please. Stay with me," I whispered through the burn in my throat.

Her face twisted. "It's time now, my love." She pulled me to her chest and squeezed. Her body was soft and warm and smelled like pine trees. Her chest shook, but I cuddled up closer. "Just know, my love, I will always love you."

"Momma..." I held her tighter. I wanted her to hold me

forever, until Daddy and Hope came back and the darkness stopped following us. But then she stepped away, and I turned cold from the inside out. She placed her right hand over my heart. "If you ever need me, this is where I'll be. Right here, real close. I will be in your heart forever. All you have to do is look."

I nodded and gripped her hand with both of mine. My tears wouldn't stop pouring.

She held her left hand up, and purple smoke swirled around her fingers. Then she pressed it to my cheek. Warmth filled me like I sat in front of a fireplace. The purple smoke circled around my face a few times before disappearing. When I looked back to Momma, her green eyes were red and puffy and full of tears. "Now, my love. Do you remember your name?"

My name? Of course I remembered my name. It was... it was... My heart raced. "No, I don't. Momma?"

"Then you're going to be just fine. I will always be proud of you. Now run, and remember, Hope is not lost." Her voice cracked. "I love you to the moon..."

"And back," I whispered.

"Now run."

I spun around and ran in the direction she pointed, toward the Tennessee wilds. I ran, like Momma told me to. I ran until the ground slanted upward and trees covered the sky. I ran until the silence was so loud it buzzed in my ears like bumblebees.

My foot caught on something, and I crashed to the ground. I got to my knees and coughed until I could breathe normally. I crawled over and leaned back against a tree to hide for a little while. I pulled my knees up to my chest and wrapped my arms around myself. I wanted Momma. I wanted Daddy. I wanted to go home. But it was all gone now. I was alone. I just wanted someone to hold me and make me feel better. Someone to make me stop crying. Someone to protect me from the darkness. I rubbed my chest over my heart. Momma said she'd always be in there, but I wanted her out here with me.

I sat in the dark, under the trees, saying the words Momma said to me over and over so I wouldn't forget. *Tennessee wilds will protect me, go to Eden, the Goddess will send guidance, and Hope was not lost.*

The sky around me had just turned a yellow color when something bit my arm. I screamed in pain and looked down. Halfway between my wrist and my elbow, a trail of fire burned into my skin. The pain got stronger and stronger until I couldn't stop screaming.

"Hey! What's wrong?"

I wanted to look up at the sound of a man's voice, but the pain was too strong. The man kept talking to me, but I couldn't hear the words.

It took me a few tries before I finally yelled, "My arm!"

Large, warm hands grabbed ahold of the arm I clutched. "Okay, let me see."

"It hurts!"

"I know." His voice was soft and friendly, but firm. It reminded me of Daddy's, and it helped calm me down. "Let me see."

I coughed and let the man pull my arm away from my body to look. "Please, make it stop," I cried.

"I'll see what I can do." The man gasped. "Goddess, almighty."

*Goddess?* Momma said the Goddess would send help. I looked up. The man had yellow eyes and yellow hair the same color as Momma's. That made me a little warm inside. "Can you make it stop?"

The man smiled like I was his favorite person. Momma used to look at me like that. He wrapped both hands around my arm. The pain got a little better. "Just breathe through it. It's almost over."

"It still hurts," I cried.

"I know it does. Count to ten with me, okay?" He squeezed my arm tighter, and it made it hurt a little less. "One..."

"Two..."

"Three..."

We counted together up to ten. By the time we were done, the pain had completely vanished. The man pulled his hands back. I took a deep breath then peeked down at my arm and gasped. The letters I and V were written on my skin in black and took up my whole arm.

"What...what is that?" I looked up to the man with yellow eyes. "What is it?"

The man smiled so wide it crinkled his eyes. "It means the Goddess has chosen you."

"Chosen...me? For what?"

"To be an important and powerful witch." The man held his left arm out and pushed up his long sleeve to reveal the letters V and III. "Look. I have one too."

I felt my eyes go wide. I glanced back and forth between our arms. "The Goddess chose you too?"

"Yes. She chooses a group of us who are special to her. This means you and I are a team. We're family now."

"We're family now?" I looked at him. He had huge shoulders, bigger than Daddy's, and his arms had lots of muscles. He might've been scary, but he smiled so much it made me feel safe. If he was my family, he'd be able to protect me.

"We sure are," he said with a big smile. "What is your name, son?"

"I don't know. I don't remember."

The man frowned but then he shrugged and smiled again. I liked when he smiled. It made me want to do it too. "Well, what would you like it to be?"

*How do I pick a name?* Then I remembered Momma's words. *Tennessee wilds will protect you.* "Tennessee Wilds."

"Well, hello, Tennessee. It's nice to meet you. My

name is Kessler Bishop." Kessler smiled real wide. "Do you know how old you are?"

I frowned and thought real hard. I couldn't remember much, but for a second I pictured a cake with five candles on it. "I think I'm five."

"Five? Well, Tennessee, you are very brave."

I didn't feel brave. What did brave feel like? "I'm scared and all alone."

Kessler's smile widened until his cheeks were pink. He put his big hand on my shoulder and squeezed. It felt nice, like Momma's hugs. "You're not alone anymore, son."

# CHAPTER ONE

## TWELVE YEARS LATER...

I stopped next to the base of a tree and crouched. The rough bark under my fingertips calmed my racing mind, anchoring me in the darkness. After thirty nonstop minutes of fighting, my chest should've burned and my breathing should've been ragged, but my body buzzed with power. I only paused to rein my energy in and focus.

Thunder rolled over my head like waves crashing on the shore. Rain had yet to fall, but the heavy blanket of clouds blocked the moon from providing me any kind of assistance. My only source of light came from the glowing sword gripped in my right hand, and it lit up a three-foot radius. So basically, I had a dashing view of some shrubbery and tree trunks surrounded by a wall of blackness. Despite spending most of my life in this exact part of the theme park, having my sight restricted suffocated me. I cursed and closed my eyes, letting my other senses fill in what my eyes missed.

To my right, the air was thick and smelled clean, the classic warning signs of a typical Florida summer rainstorm. The wind blowing my hair across my face was damp and cool. I figured we had about twenty minutes tops before the clouds unleashed a monsoon right on top of me.

I turned to the left and took a deep breath. A sickening sweet scent tickled my nose from nearby. I slid my hand down the tree trunk until I found the familiar wet and sticky patch. I brought my fingers up to my face and sniffed. No matter how many times I inhaled the stuff, the maple syrup-like scent always burned a path down my airways.

*Demon blood.*

We'd been chasing this particular creature through the park for half an hour to no avail. It somehow kept eluding our efforts. This thing led us into the darkest part of the park, where overgrown black olive trees lined one paved stretch of road. How I managed to be outsmarted by a demon in my home territory I'd never know. My pride didn't appreciate it.

*Focus, Tennessee.*

Even with the moonlight, the branches overhead created a tunnel effect. Fortunately, I knew this park ground-up by memory. Unfortunately, this meant I knew the demon was a mere hundred feet away from the Gap back to its realm. We needed to act fast.

The bushes behind me rustled and twigs snapped. Deja-vu had me spinning on my toes and pouncing before I'd consciously told myself to do so. However, I knew the second my fingers touched something soft that it wasn't a demon. This didn't stop me from pinning the person to the ground and holding my sword up to their throat.

"Whoa, it's me!"

I sighed and gripped the front of my friend's silky shirt, using the glow from my sword to light up his face. Wide, deep sapphire eyes stared at me. His high, sharp cheekbones looked worthy of a magazine cover.

"Damn it, Royce. I thought you were smarter than this." Royce was one of my best friends, one of the guys who fought by my side the most. He should've known better. *I could've killed him.*

"And I thought you were partially human." Royce cracked a crooked, dimpled grin and shrugged, completely at ease despite the glowing sword at his throat or the warrior perched above him. "Appears we're both wrong."

I rolled my eyes and moved off him. "I am no less human than you, my friend."

Royce scoffed. "Humans, even partial humans like me, don't move like that. If you want me to believe you're human at all, I'm gonna need a blood test."

Despite the situation, I chuckled and shook my head

while resuming my crouched position beside the tree. "Guess I know what to get you for Christmas."

"Fine, but it better be gift-wrapped in cashmere."

I opened my mouth to respond when a gust of wind whipped through the trees, carrying the thick stench of maple syrup. "Royce, your cologne is calling."

Without waiting, I leapt to my feet and ran toward the smell. I held my left hand up and summoned a gust of wind, directing it through the trees and down the tunneled path. The sickening smell enclosed around me from every direction.

Royce coughed and mumbled something unintelligible. I slid to a stop and stared up at the intertwined branches. Without taking my eyes off the trees, I crouched and pulled my dagger out of my left boot. After a second of silence, leaves rustled like drops of rain were hitting them, moving farther away from us down the middle of the path.

*There you are.* I adjusted the hilt of my dagger in my fingers and threw the weapon into the trees in an arching movement.

A high-pitched shriek shot through the forest about ten feet in front of us. A large dark shadow dropped to the ground with a thud, followed by the *clink* of something metal. *Gotcha.*

"There!" Royce shouted and sprinted past me in the dark.

*He should know better.*

14

I narrowed my eyes and willed my dagger to illuminate. A soft yellow glow lit up like a firework a foot in front of Royce. He cheered and dove to tackle the spider-like demon off course, desperation making him reckless. The force of his hit sent them sliding down the pavement and rolling. I cursed as I followed them, then jumped onto the demon's back, riding his hard shell like a surfboard.

This demon was seven feet long, with eight legs full of razor-edged spikes. And Royce was pinned underneath it. Instinct made me aim my sword down but I paused. If I stabbed the demon in the wrong spot, my blade would impale Royce. If I hurt my friend... No, I couldn't even consider the possibility.

With a curse, I gritted my teeth and summoned another gust of wind. When the cool air hit, I dropped my sword, gripped the tusk-like pinchers on the demon's face, and flipped onto my back. Royce shouted in alarm as the demon went flying. I held my gaze on the demon soaring above me. A streak of lightning the color of blood shot through dark sky and slammed into the airborne demon.

*Libby.*

"Move!" Libby shouted from nearby.

I rolled to the side and jumped to my feet. With a flick of my wrist, both my sword and dagger flew through the air and landed in my open palms.

Libby continued zapping the demon with her spell

until it shrank to the size of a pit bull. Too late I realized her spell was having a unique reaction on the monster.

"Stop!" I yelled. The smaller the demon, the harder they were to catch.

The red lightning ceased, and the demon crashed to the ground. The creature rolled onto its eight legs and scurried into the trees...*right in Libby's direction.* Years of training instructed me to always kill the demon first, save friends second. I adjusted my grip on my sword. In my mind, Kessler's voice told me to take the kill shot.

Too bad I'd never been good at rules.

I planted my feet, pulled my right arm back, and threw my sword like a javelin. The glowing blade soared through the air like a missile before diving into the ground at Libby's feet. The earth exploded and cracked, sending the demon and Libby flying in opposite directions. I ran forward and yanked my sword from the ground. Up ahead, the demon scrambled back to its eight-foot height.

"That should've killed it." Libby cursed and shot at the demon with her lightning, shrinking it a little bit more. Her light brown eyebrows were scrunched low over narrowed hazel eyes.

"No, stop," I shouted. "Too small and we'll never catch it."

"He's on the move!" Royce yelled from ahead of them. He looked scraped up but was on his feet nonetheless.

The demon hissed and sped off toward the Gap. I

cursed and sprinted after it, leaving Libby in the dust. I pushed to my maximum speed, passing by Royce in a blur. The damn demon seemed to be getting faster the smaller he was. By the time I caught up to it, we were only twenty feet from the Gap. Thanks to the ornate lanterns hanging from posts every five feet in this area, I had no problem seeing just how close we were to it.

I dove like I was in the World Series and slammed into the side of the demon, burying my sword into its side. The creature screamed and rolled. Inky black blood sprayed like a firehose, burning my skin everywhere it landed.

I placed my palms on the concrete and directed my power into the earth. The world trembled all around me. Lamp posts and signs crashed to the ground. Water splashed off the fountain ten feet away. I needed one of my weapons to kill it, but my sword was lodged in the demon's belly and my dagger was taking its sweet time responding to my call. I felt the pull in my gut, the tickle in my fingertips. I just needed to stall. Out of the corner of my eye, I spotted Royce and Libby crossing the bridge and entering the French Square. The demon seemed unable, or afraid, to move while the ground shook.

"Yeah, definitely gonna need that blood test," Royce said once he caught up. He bent over with his hands on his knees, gasping for air. "I think you're getting less and less human."

I rolled my eyes, although I didn't miss the fact he had

a point. I wasn't even breathing heavy. "Does that smart mouth of yours know how to kill this thing?"

"My mouth knows how to do a lot of things." Royce smirked. He grabbed ahold of the iron fence next to him and tried to stand. "You mind, bro?"

I... *What?* I wasn't sure what he'd just proposed until I spotted Libby crawling up the path behind Royce. *Oh. Right.*

I took one hand off the ground so my friends could move freely and kept the other shaking the demon. "Sorry. We need to trap it."

"Your sword should've killed it. My spell should've killed it." Libby jogged over to the right, closer to the ten-foot-tall fountain. Her little double-edged dagger was gripped tightly in her right hand. With her left, she directed bolts of bloodred lightning to block the demon's path like a wall. "How the hell *do* we kill it?"

"Do we have to kill it?" Royce asked, still holding on to the fence, but he appeared to be breathing normal again. "I mean, if it wants to go home, let it go. Good riddance."

"It will just come back." Libby moved so she was on the opposite side of the demon from me.

"Yeah, but in the meantime, we can figure out how to kill it. Right?" Royce moved to the left until the three of us formed a triangle around it. He had his dagger, which was the size of his forearm, out and ready.

I sighed. I wanted to go along with the idea. I really

did. The Gap was right there. The three of us could easily chase it back to its own dimension and worry about it another day. I was sleep deprived, starving, and not interested in being stuck out in a thunderstorm.

*Tempting, so tempting.* But then I remembered Cassandra's instructions when she called to tell me there was a demon loose outside the park.

I cursed for the eight hundredth time that night. "No, Cassandra said we had to kill it. She specifically said not to let this demon get through the Gap."

"Did she say why?" Libby asked. Her voice was weakening from the energy it took her to use her spell. The soft curve of her round face didn't match the aggressive attitude.

"Unfortunately not."

Royce cursed.

"Do we have to listen?"

I frowned and looked over to Libby, who was now on her knees with her hands outstretched. On her left forearm, the Roman numerals XV were burned into her skin. *The Devil.* It wasn't her fault; it was her Card after all. Temptation was the name of her game. *This is why Kessler sends her with you. You're the only one he trusts with her.*

*But she has a valid point. Do we have to listen?*

"I don't wanna answer to Kessler when we don't listen," Royce responded.

"I don't want to be killed by a giant spider," Libby

snapped. "Besides, Tennessee should be the one telling Kessler what to do."

*What?*

Royce ran his free hand through his jet-black hair. He looked over at me and shrugged. "She has a point, Emperor."

My stomach rolled. I glanced down at the Roman numeral IV on my arm, the mark of The Emperor. Out of all twenty-two Cards, The Emperor was *meant* to lead. Supreme ruler. I was supposed to sit on the throne of the Coven in my armor and reign. And I could've, too, if I wanted. Despite being seventeen.

But I didn't want to. At all. In any way. The idea of being in charge made my spine tingle and heartrate skyrocket.

Royce cleared his throat. "It's your call, Emperor. We've got your back."

I glared at the demon while I deliberated. Cassandra never led me astray. The Goddess chose her for a reason; she must've had a reason. It may have been my natural right to lead, but it wasn't my role to question our spiritual advisor. "Cassandra said we had to kill it. So, we're going to kill it."

"Okay...how?"

I glanced over at Libby, who was barely holding herself upright. Royce stood, ready to fight, but he'd taken a beating already. "Okay, Royce, go stand in front of the

Gap. Hold your ground. Do not let the demon, or me, go through it."

Royce blanched. "Or you?"

I nodded. "Libby, on my move, drop your shield and take cover."

Libby nodded, her hazel eyes dark with fatigue. Even from fifteen feet away, her skin looked pale. Royce limped over to stand in front of the fountain.

This demon wasn't like the other demons and Gap jumpers we fought, which meant I wouldn't be able to kill it the same way. I had an idea, a crazy idea, but it was all I had. Now I had to hope it didn't backfire and get my friends hurt. I could handle just about anything except being the reason my friends got hurt.

Royce got into place, holding a strong fighting stance. "Ready, boss."

*Don't call me that.*

I turned and met Libby's gaze. "When I run forward, drop it."

Libby nodded. "You got it, boss."

*Please stop calling me that.*

I pushed those thoughts away and summoned all of my power to the surface until my entire body glowed brighter than a full moon. Once at full strength, I held my right hand out and mentally called for my dagger. Within seconds, the cool metal hit my palm, and I tightened my grip around the hilt. I removed my left hand from the ground, and the earth immediately settled. The demon stumbled and tripped, its eight legs struggling to remain upright.

*Now the crazy part.*

*Please let this work.*

I held my palm out toward the fountain and shot a bolt of pure white energy into the pool at the base. Water and coins shot into the night sky. The demon raced toward the Gap behind Royce, dodging quarters and slipping in the new puddles. Just as I expected, the fairy spirits guarding the Gap sprang from their hiding spots and dove toward the demon. The spider-like monster reared up on its back four legs. I dove toward the creature and buried my dagger in the back of its neck. It shrieked and flipped over, but I was faster. I reached down, grabbed the hilt of my sword protruding from the demon's side, and sliced through its body.

Under its tusks, the demon had a humanoid face with beady red eyes and sparkly white teeth. It snarled and coughed. "You'll never close the Gap without the tool," it hissed.

I was so taken back by it being able to speak that I didn't realize what it said until it was too late. One of its eight legs ripped something off from around its neck and threw it right into the Gap opening.

I leaped forward. It might've been a trick, but we couldn't risk it. Closing the Gap had been our species' main focus since everything went down in Salem centuries ago. I had no idea what the tool was, but I watched it fly through the air like a shooting star.

*I'm never going to catch it.*

The demon wrapped one of its legs around my foot and yanked me back. The object crossed into the Gap when a little pink hand reached through the hole and snatched it. In a flash of a second, I recognized the flutter of luminescent wings and a dash of bright red hair before the fairy disappeared from sight with whatever the demon threw now clutched in her hand.

My back hit the water of the fountain's pool with a splash. I rolled and pushed the barely living demon under until the water turned black and bubbled. The fairy spirits hissed and dove toward me, razor claws outstretched. With my sword in one hand and a dagger in the other, I spun and sliced my weapons at anything that moved. Fairies screamed and ducked away from the bright glow radiating from me. Within seconds, there was nothing but silence and my pounding heart.

Still, I wasn't tired, wasn't even breathing heavy. My heart beat with adrenaline, the rush of my power, and excitement of action. I spun around in circles, looking for another fight, but the night was calm. Glittery fairy dust shimmered in the air around the fountain and the pool's water looked like black sludge, but the demon was gone. Thunder rolled and lightning cracked through the sky, although I couldn't have said if it was from *me* or Mother Nature. I turned, searching for the only living fairy the theme park had, but she was nowhere to be seen.

*We've never been able to catch her.*

"Forget the blood test..."

I turned toward the familiar voice and found Royce's wide sapphire eyes staring. I frowned. "What?"

"Ya know, when you glow like that, your eyes almost look the same color."

"What are you getting at?" I scowled down at him. I understood the words he'd said, just not why he said them.

"Though the green one gets brighter than the blue one," Royce mumbled.

"Did you hit your head? What are you trying to say?" Everyone knew I had different colored eyes: the left was blue, and the right was green. It was the first thing people noticed, usually.

Royce shook his head. "No way in hell you're human."

I climbed out of the fountain pool and held my palm out for Royce. "So, this means you just want cashmere?"

Royce chuckled and let himself be lifted to his feet. "Or silk. I'm not picky."

"Yes, you are."

"I know." Royce grinned. He didn't seem terribly injured, but there were definitely going to be some marks to heal.

I shook my head and raced to where our friend was on

the ground. I crouched and reached out to...*to do what?* I wasn't sure what to do to help. Why was she so still? But then I saw her chest rising and falling, and I sighed with relief. She was alive. Thank the Goddess. "Libby, are you okay?"

"I still prefer the blue, Royce." She sat up and brushed some hair out of her face, her light brown hair barely holding on to her trademark side braid. A lamp post had fallen behind her and landed on her left foot, pinning it to the ground. I lifted the metal off of her, earning me a flirty smile in return.

I frowned, then my cell phone rang from inside my pocket. When I pulled it out, I found my adoptive father's face filling the screen. I took a deep breath to make sure I sounded calm and collected. I answered and hit the button to put him on speakerphone. "Hello, Father dearest."

"Are you okay? Where is it? Did the demon get through the Gap?"

"I'm fine, we're all fine. No, I killed it. Like Cassandra asked me to." I looked around. "This theme park isn't okay, though."

Royce limped over and leaned on my shoulder. "Yeah, the Sapiens are going to freak out when they see this."

Kessler sighed but I could tell he was relieved. "I'll see to the mess. Willow, Cassandra, and I are already on the way. You three get home."

"No argument here." Royce laughed, but the wince told me it hurt to do so.

"I'm calling a meeting tomorrow at noon at our spot." Kessler mumbled something to someone on his side of the call. "Tenn, you good to drive the three of you home?"

"Yeah, no problem. I feel pretty good right now."

Royce scoffed. "Because you ain't human."

"Tenn, try and get some sleep. I'll be home soon."

"Yes, sir." I ended the call and put my phone back in my pocket.

Royce stood straight and smiled. Normally, whoever smelt it dealt it, meaning whoever made the mess cleaned the mess, so getting the clear to go home was a blessing.

"Tennessee?"

I looked down to where Libby sat on the ground with a rather swollen-looking ankle. "Yeah?"

She batted her eyelashes and smiled. "Will you carry me to the car? Please?"

Behind her, Royce rolled his eyes and made a gagging gesture. I ignored him and crouched down. Libby wrapped her arms around my neck the second I got close enough.

She beamed up at me, her cheeks flushed. "You're such a sweetheart."

Royce scoffed and shook his head, disgusted by the damsel-in-distress act. I shrugged one shoulder and smiled. Damsel or not, she'd hurt her foot enough to warrant not walking on it right away. Carrying her was the least I could do.

But the look in Libby's hazel eyes and the way she licked her bottom lip told me she had other ideas in mind. The question was, why didn't I want to take her up on them?

# CHAPTER TWO

S he placed her right hand over my heart. "If you ever need me, this is where I'll be. Right here, real close. I will be in your heart forever. All you have to do is look."

I nodded and gripped her hand with both of mine. The tears wouldn't stop pouring.

She held her left hand up, and purple smoke swirled around her fingers. Then she pressed it to my cheek. Warmth filled me like I sat in front of a fireplace. The purple smoke circled around my face a few times before disappearing. When I looked back to Momma, her green eyes were red and puffy and full of tears. "Now, my love. Do you remember your name?"

My name? Of course I remembered my name. It was...it was... My heart raced. "No, I don't. Momma?"

"Then you're going to be just fine. I will always be

*proud of you. Now run, and remember, Hope is not lost."* Her voice cracked. *"I love you to the moon..."*

"Tennessee!"

I shot upright and shouted, "And back!"

My heart slammed against my chest, beating out of control and making my entire body tremble with adrenaline. I was in the back of my Jeep, with my legs bent in weird directions and one bare foot hanging out the window. The leather jacket I'd used to block out any and all light dropped to my lap. The sunlight accosted me from every direction.

*It was just a dream.*

*Again.*

If I could even call it a dream. In actuality, it was a memory, the oldest one I had, from the last time I saw my mother. The only thing I really remembered of my mother, and it wasn't much. I hadn't dreamed about that night in years, yet in the last few weeks, it'd been almost a nightly occurrence. Was my brain trying to tell me something or simply torturing me?

The door my right foot hung out of flew open, and my heel slammed against the side of the car. The new angle had my left leg screaming in duress. Okay, so maybe I was too big to sleep in the back of a Jeep Wrangler. Maybe sleeping in my car had been a horrible idea. *Note to self: just sleep on the sand next time.* Or my bed, actually. A string of curses left my lips.

"Tennessee."

My eyes finally focused on the moving object in front of me. Cassandra's pale face glared at me. Her red, pursed lips perfectly matched the red eyebrow arched in frustration.

"Alive yet?"

I managed to get my body into a proper seated position, but the onslaught of light made me drop my head. "Debatable."

She chuckled. "What's happening in here this morning, Tenn?"

"I didn't want to be late for the meeting, so I drove over here to wait."

"Seriously?"

I shrugged and it made my neck crack. "Kessler hates when I'm late."

"Right, and he'll be thrilled with your solution." She laughed again. "We all heard your cell phone alarm, except for you. Come on. It's time."

With a heavy sigh, I dragged myself out of the Jeep and stumbled a few times until my legs got the wake-up memo. The asphalt burned my bare feet, but it helped get my brain into action. I lifted each arm one at a time and sniffed my pits. *Yeah, maybe I should've stayed home.*

Cassandra whistled. "Dude, you look like hell."

"Thanks, I found the look on Pinterest." I smiled and yanked my dirty shirt off, then threw it inside the Jeep. I'd pick it up later. Eventually. I plucked a shirt off the floor, smelled it, and threw it to join the other. It took three more tries before I found a shirt clean enough to wear in public.

When I looked up, I found Cassandra shaking her head and laughing. "C'mon, pretty boy. Here, I have a feeling you'll need these." My black sunglasses dangled from her red-freckled fingers.

Twenty-two seconds later, my toes sank into the powdery sand. I paused and frowned down at my bare feet. *Did I need to put shoes back on?* My brain seemed to be in a bit of a fog, and I wasn't sure how to shake it. I looked up to search for my Coven and hissed when the sun pierced through my black sunglasses and stung my eyes. If I didn't know any better, I'd think I was becoming a vampire. I needed to talk to Kessler and Cassandra about why I struggled with fatigue and sensory sensitivity all of a sudden. Normally I recharged fairly quickly. Not to mention the recurring dreams, although I was in no hurry to bring those up. They'd want to know how these dreams made me feel and ask a string of personally introspective questions. The mere idea made me cringe with horror.

I took a deep breath of hot, sticky air and groaned. Even the breeze blowing through my hair was warm. Sadly, Florida's summer heat had only just begun. In a matter of days, I'd be seeing triple digits and puddles of sweat in my clothes. I reached up and brushed my long black hair out of my face, pulling it back and tying it into a knot on top of my head. It was probably, definitely, far past time for a trim, but I'd lost the desire to combat the speed at which the wavy strands grew. *Until then, man bun for the win.*

"Wow, with six seconds to spare. I'm impressed, Tennessee."

I glanced up ahead to where my adoptive father's voice had come from and found him eyeing me with an amused grin. Kessler was an intimidating sight, standing six foot five with the widest shoulders I'd ever seen on a person. I was a pretty big guy for my age, two inches over six foot and a solid two hundred pounds, but my father still had at least fifty pounds on me. He had a short blond buzz cut and eyes the color of liquid gold. So basically, we looked exactly alike. *Heavy sarcasm.*

"Eight seconds," I corrected him. My voice sounded like gravel to my own ears, so it was probably even worse to everyone else.

"Does it count if he's not alive?" Cooper shouted from somewhere in the group.

"Hey, I've got a clean shirt on."

"Yeah, it took him four tries to find it though." Cassandra elbowed me gently in the side then walked over to a lavish purple blanket behind Kessler and sat. "And by clean he means it smelled better than the others."

She wasn't wrong. I shrugged. "I'm here."

"Apparently you've been here a while. We'll discuss

this at great length later." Kessler shook his head and laughed. He gestured toward the rest of the group who sat on blankets in a semicircle around him. "Take a seat, son. We have things to discuss."

I nodded and glanced to my right where the rest of my crew waited patiently. Fourteen pairs of eyes looked up to me expectantly. I didn't know what they were expecting me to do though. *Or maybe I do.* These people were my extended family, specifically chosen out of our entire race of witches by the Goddess herself to lead our society. The Cards, as we were commonly referred. Twenty-two Cards made up the Coven which ruled our kind, and fifteen of us lived in Florida. *And they want me to lead.*

I sighed. *Don't think about it right now.* I strolled over to where my brother Cooper sat and plopped down beside him. I may not have looked a damn thing like my adoptive father, but Cooper was practically a carbon copy, just younger and with light green eyes. "Did I miss anything?"

"Yeah, it's called summer," Easton said with a wide grin. His bright blue eyes were the same color as the sky above us. Similar to Kessler and Cooper, Easton had naturally platinum blond hair, except he wore his a little longer on the top to give the ladies something to hold on to. His words, not mine. His arm was draped around a pretty, raven-haired Lily. "Maybe you should try wearing a color other than black."

"Be happy I have clothes on."

Libby raised her hand from behind Easton like they were sitting in class. "Do we have to be happy about that?"

Everyone laughed and tossed handfuls of sand in Libby's direction, moaning a variety of discouraging remarks. Like a switch had been flipped, the group spiraled into theatrics, and sand soared through the air in every direction.

"I still say blue," Libby said under her breath while sand blasted her face.

*Blue what?*

"Enough," Kessler snapped and the sand froze in the air. "Coven meeting first, sand fight second. Deal?"

He waited until everyone nodded and collected themselves before beginning. "As you know, we had an encounter with a special kind of creature last night. This demon overheard Cassandra and I talking and learned some information we couldn't risk getting to the other realms. This is why it was imperative you killed it."

"Is that why we're here? To discuss why we have to kill demons?" Libby asked, part sarcasm, part genuine curiosity.

"We actually have a more pressing issue about last night." Kessler exchanged a quick glance with Cassandra. Hesitation from him was never a good sign. Especially when he turned his pointed gaze directly at me. "Tennessee? Royce and Libby filled us in on everything, except they claim the demon said something to you."

*Ah, crap.* I had every intention of bringing it up, but not in front of everyone. The last thing we needed was talk about Salem's prophecy and closing the Gap. However, everyone was staring at me. Waiting. It would be wrong to lie to them. *Wouldn't it?* Yes. Yes, it would.

I shook the idea away and cleared my throat. *Here goes nothing.* "It said, 'you'll never close the Gap without the tool.'"

Questions fired at rapid pace. "Did it say what the tool was?" "Did it have the tool?" "Like a literal tool?" "A tool like an amulet?" I sorted through them silently, trying to decide how to answer. Giving these guys all the information would be bad news. I needed to talk it out in private with Kessler and Cassandra.

"Easton is a tool," Braison joked, speaking up for the first time all day.

"Tennessee?" Kessler pointed his finger at Easton to stop him from tackling Braison.

"No, it didn't say what the tool was." Not technically a lie. I slid my sunglasses on top of my head and pinched the bridge of my nose. When I looked up, I caught Kessler's eye, moved my gaze to Cassandra, then returned it back to Kessler. Then I lied and hoped he'd understand why. "No, it didn't have the tool. I don't know much more than any of you."

Silence.

"Well, I might." Cassandra smiled but it looked more

like a deranged serial killer than cheerful. Her emerald green eyes were way too wide and bloodshot to have any good news. She stood and brushed the white powdery sand off her red-freckled legs. "The Goddess paid me a little visit last night and left us a present."

My stomach turned. Cassandra was the Hierophant. Of all the Cards, she was the one most connected to the Goddess and served as our spiritual advisor. Our Priest, practically holy herself. The Goddess communicated with Cassandra frequently for a multitude of reasons, but when She left a present, it only meant one thing. A quest. Her presents were the lines of prophecy to aid in our mission.

I already knew where this quest would lead. At least now I knew why Cassandra wore a long-sleeved shirt at noon in the summer. She wanted to hide the prophecy until we were ready.

Cassandra stepped forward so everyone could see then slid her left sleeve up to her elbow. A giant letter V in black ink marked her pale forearm in the exact place we all had our Marks. The Hierophant, tarot card number five. But we'd all seen it before. What we focused on today were the four lines of words written on her skin in an elegant black scroll.

She read it out loud without looking. *"Seek the tool from thieving hands. First ally with those between the lands. To mend the bond between them all, listen for the vengeful Fallen's call."*

I stared at her arm. *Thieving hands.* She knew. The Goddess knew the little fairy had grabbed the item before it disappeared through the Gap. Although I didn't know why this surprised me. I had no idea what any of the rest of it meant, but I was right to keep some details to myself. I sat there in silence, ignoring all the noise and commotion around me, and tried to recount my steps from the night before. I needed to remember every detail from when the demon spoke to when the supposed tool vanished from my sight.

"Tennessee?" A large, warm hand landed on my right shoulder, and I about jumped out of my skin. "Easy, son."

I hung my head between my knees and counted to three to calm my racing heart. Kessler's hand gripped my shoulder tighter, and it helped a little. When I picked my head back up, I found we were alone on the beach except for Cassandra and Cooper.

*What the hell?* "Where did everyone else go?"

Cassandra, Cooper, and Kessler all exchanged anxious glances.

"What?"

Kessler frowned. "Son, I sent everyone home about ten minutes ago. You've been staring at nothing since. Why don't you tell us what really happened?"

My shoulders dropped with relief. He'd gotten my subtle hint and wasn't mad I'd withheld from him. At least not yet. I took a deep breath then went into a detailed description of what happened. I paid extra attention to the item the demon threw. "I still don't know what the item is, but I'm assuming it was the tool."

Cooper's blond eyebrows dropped low over his light green eyes. He scratched the back of his head. "We have to find this fairy."

"Last thing we need is for everyone to go hunting for her." I looked to Kessler.

He nodded. "You're right. The panic will make everyone restless and reckless. This could lead to accidents. The four of us will have to try and find it ourselves, although Tennessee is the only one who has seen it."

"I didn't get much of a look."

"Cooper and I will go to the park now," Cassandra volunteered. "We will start the search. Kessler, now more than ever, we need to get them trained and ready."

"Agreed. Come by before open house tonight so we can regroup." Kessler started to ramble off a bunch of things, but Cassandra held her palms up to stop him. I'd never seen someone with freckles on their palms before I met her.

She smiled and nodded her head toward me. Her emerald eyes were sharper now than they'd been a few minutes ago. "You need to take this one home. Give him some real food and the tea I gave you the other day, then put him to bed. He's so drained he can barely withstand sunlight."

I sighed. I didn't even need to ask her or voice my concerns out loud. She *knew.*

Kessler took a long look at me, then nodded. "C'mon, son. Let's get you home."

I climbed to my feet. My whole body ached and cracked with every movement. Sleep sounded blissful. So did food. Before I followed my father to the car, I turned toward Cassandra to tell her something about the fairy but found her eyeing me oddly.

I narrowed my eyes. "What?"

She frowned and cocked her head to the side. "I had an interesting dream about you last night."

My heart sank faster than the *Titanic.* The Hierophant dreaming about you rarely meant something good. "Do tell."

"It was strange." She shook her head, and her red curls bounced over her shoulders. "You were chasing something down a river, and you just kept screaming for hope."

# CHAPTER THREE

"You don't look any more rested than you did seven hours ago, brother."

I sighed and leaned against the student services counter next to an obnoxious sign saying WELCOME BACK TO GULF SHORES HIGH! I didn't bother glaring at Cooper. From anyone else, yes, I would glare. Coop meant it from a place of concern, even if he sucked at putting the words together. "You say the sweetest things to me, brother."

Cooper ignored this and crossed the hallway to where I leaned. He glanced over both shoulders to make sure no one in the empty sitting area was listening. "Didn't Kessler give you anything?"

"He gave me lots of things." Including a lecture on taking better care of myself. Normally I kept myself and my room crisp and clean, but lately I simply lacked the energy. And now I had a matter of days until my junior year of high school started. Not to mention the quest, which only held the fate of the world in its hands. No pressure.

Something in my gut told me to brace myself. The other shoe was about to drop. To quote the great Tom Petty, "the waiting is the hardest part."

"Tennessee," Cooper said with that low voice he made when he wanted to hide his emotions. "Give yourself a break. You're not in charge here."

I sighed and met his pale green eyes. "Tell that to everyone else."

Cooper nodded but dropped the subject. If there was anyone less comfortable talking about their emotions than me, it was my adoptive brother. I used to wonder the nature versus nurture aspect of our similar personalities before I decided I didn't really care about the whys. Cooper was my best friend by choice, not because we grew up in the same house.

We were silent a few minutes, both lost in our own stress, until the doors off to our left opened and a group of rosy-cheeked girls entered the building. The sun shining through the open doorway made me cringe. Still, I would've preferred to be out there with the chirping birds and fresh air than in here with lemon-scented cleaner stinging my sinuses.

The girls giggled and walked in front of us to the guidance counselor's sign-in sheet. Their laughter echoed down the empty hallway. Kessler would've chastised me for being rude and not saying hello, but I preferred the incoming freshmen females to be too afraid to talk to me. It was easier that way. Less questions.

"Maybe you should...ya know..." Cooper nodded his blond head in the girls' direction. They were only fifteen feet away, so I was glad he'd dropped the volume of his voice.

I arched one eyebrow at him. "Why don't you?"

He sighed. "Fair enough."

The guidance counselor's door opened next to where the girls stood, still giggling in my direction. Kessler stepped into the doorway, waved back at our counselor, then crossed the hallway to join us.

"Sorry, boys." Kessler's deep voice was a welcome reprieve from myself, Cooper's concern, and my group of admirers. "Took a little longer than planned."

I opened my mouth to ask a question when I spotted two class schedules in his hand. They were bright pink and had the school's dragon logo printed on the top. Every student had gotten one tonight. *Wait a second...* My schedule was in my back pocket. Cooper was currently using his as a fan.

I frowned. Did he get new ones for us? "Whose schedules are those?"

"Come on, I've told everyone to meet us at the lunch tables outside before open house starts." Kessler completely ignored my question. He turned and waved us along.

With every step I took, my sense of dread enlarged. By the time we got to the outside lunch tables, my palms were sweaty and my heart beat like I'd run a marathon. It was only seven o'clock, so the Florida sun sat bright and shiny in a cloudless blue sky. The temperature in my car had said ninety-nine when we arrived thirty minutes ago, so it was probably only ninety-seven degrees out now. Sweat broke out over my forehead and on the back of my neck. I reached up and pulled my long hair into a knot on top of my head to let that refreshing warm breeze cool me off. *Maybe Easton had a point. I wear a lot of black for a Floridian in the summer.*

Our Coven sat in various positions, some like normal humans at the tables while some lounged on the massive oak tree branches like leopards. To the outside world, they looked relaxed and a little weird. But I saw the tension in their bodies and the way their dark eyes anxiously bounced from shadow to shadow. Their hands idled near whatever weapon they chose to stash on their bodies. I looked to Cassandra for some kind of clue, except her gaze was locked on the prophecy written on her arm.

Kessler cleared his throat. "Hey, everyone, thanks for meeting me here early. Since our chat this afternoon, some news has been made official, and so I need to share it with you."

The knots in my gut tightened and twisted. Cooper chose to sit on one of the table's benches beside Kessler. I barely managed to stand still next to him. It took everything in me not to pace like a caged lion. My normally raucous crew sat in perfect silence...waiting.

"I'm not going to sugarcoat this... We're here to discuss the twins."

There was a collective gasp, a chorus of audible shock. Someone fell out of the tree behind Kessler, but I didn't look to see who it was. Out of the corner of my eye, I saw everyone turn to their neighbor with incredulous faces, like they hoped they'd heard wrong. There were whispers and wild hand gestures.

I swallowed down my own unease and stepped closer to Kessler. "The twins... As in the original pair?" *Please say yes. Please, please say yes. Please.*

Kessler paused a beat and then shook his head. He held his golden stare level. "I mean the new pair."

*The twins. Salem's prophecy is finally here.*

Cooper cursed under his breath and ran a hand over his buzzed, blond head. "What about them?"

I reached over and squeezed my adoptive brother's shoulder. He stood pin straight with his arms locked at his sides and his hands in fists. The muscles in his biceps flexed. His lips were pressed into a hard line. Kessler was

Cooper's uncle and had technically adopted Cooper sixteen years ago after his real parents delivered a set of twin baby girls. Cooper still felt responsible for the outcome of his younger sisters' prophecy, and every day his attitude darkened a little more.

"They're coming." Kessler raised both hands in the air to ward off questions. "As you know, the spells we placed on them as newborns will only last until their sixteenth birthday...next month."

A chorus of violent curses rippled through the crew.

I frowned and cleared my throat. To everyone else in our Coven, my father had dropped a bomb, destroying whatever plans they had for the rest of summer and the foreseeable future. For me? If I had to name the emotion running through me, I'd call it relief. Living with biological family members of the twins meant I heard about them practically every week for the last twelve years.

I only needed to know a little more. "How does the process work? Will their powers just come out full force or slowly?"

"What kind of powers are we expecting them to have, anyway?" Easton asked, his light blue eyes narrowed. His platinum blond hair was wild and sticking out in several directions like he'd been tugging at it.

Cooper groaned and put his head in his tan hands. I understood why. There was a tiny detail the Coven leaders kept secret from the rest of the race, including the other

Cards. For everyone's sake. The lid was about to be blown off. I gritted my teeth and braced myself.

"Well, they've got to have some power," Henley said, "Otherwise they wouldn't be able to close the Gap in Salem. Right, Cassandra?"

Everyone turned to look at Cassandra, who'd been quietly leaning against the base of the tree. Her bright red hair was tied up in a messy bun on top of her head and her shirt definitely had a mustard stain on the left shoulder. She gnawed on her bottom lip for a moment before turning her glance up to Kessler. "It's time."

Kessler sighed and nodded. "The twins were born with Marks."

Deafening silence.

"WHAT?" Royce shouted. He'd been uncharacteristically quiet so far.

"Are you saying they're Cards?" Henley asked. No one would've been surprised to hear she was Royce's older sister since they had the same sapphire eyes and jet-black hair. Both had lean bodies, high cheekbones, and impeccable style. Although Henley had the whole goth vibe going, and Royce dressed like a supermodel. Still...

On the outside, Kessler looked like we were making weekend plans. He was calm and quiet. His voice didn't waver or rise louder. He gave absolutely nothing away, and no one would know if he was silently freaking out inside. Unless you were me, then you'd know his arms were held behind his back to hide the slight tremor in his fingers when he got nervous. Or the way his jaw popped when he wasn't speaking because he was grinding his teeth.

"Yes," he said. "They're Cards, which means they are one of us. The Coven must embrace them as we would any other new Card."

"Wait, hold up, Kess." Easton raised his hand. "Which Cards are they?"

"I thought all the Cards were taken," Henley said from the back.

"I do not have a good feeling about this," Royce mumbled.

"Two of our twenty-two Coven members had fallen during an attack at exactly the right time, or should I say the wrong time. Not surprisingly, the Goddess chose the twins to fill these roles."

"Kessler...which roles did they fill?" Henley asked. Something about the sharp expression in her sapphire eyes and the pointed look she exchanged with her brother told me she'd already figured it out and was hoping he'd prove her wrong. "Kessler?"

Kessler ran a hand through his cropped blond hair, a nervous tick his nephew Cooper had picked up. "My nieces have been Marked Empress and High Priestess."

The group erupted into absolute chaos. Wild exclamations of horror, violent curses, and variations of "how the hell are we supposed to contain them?"

echoed around me. I understood their reaction. Hell, I'd had a similar one when I found out. The entire race of witches depended on the twenty-two Cards who made up the Coven to protect everyone. Of those twenty-two, three Cards had more power than the others...

The High Priestess.

The Empress.

*...and The Emperor.*

I sighed and avoided the stares of my friends as they realized *I* was their answer. Instead, I glanced down at my left arm to where the Roman numeral four stained my skin. The Mark of The Emperor. I remembered the moment it appeared...the pain, the fear, the confusion... *Kessler.* I looked up at the only father I remembered and hoped he saw the rising panic in my eyes.

"All right, all right, all right," Kessler yelled over the noise. "This responsibility does not lie only on Tennessee's shoulders. Each and every one of us has an equal part to play."

"What's the plan?" Cooper asked, his voice low and strained.

"They're moving here after their birthday to start school with you. We'll have a better plan when it gets closer. For now, it's my job to get the rest of you ready."

"Can you be a little less cryptic?" Royce mumbled loud enough for everyone to hear.

"Let's not stress with details yet. We're going to switch up your training a little bit..." He turned his gaze to me.

I clenched my teeth. *I already don't like this.*

"You're all going to be training with Tennessee this summer."

More groans and curses, including my own, although I kept mine silent. I probably should've been offended by their reaction, but I was too busy agreeing with them. I had the most power, the best fighting skills, the most abilities out of the group... It made perfect, logical sense. And I hated that I had to admit it, even to myself.

"Practice is over. In order to be your best, you must be trained by the best." Kessler held up his palms to ward off questions. Again. "Cassandra and I assessed your weaknesses for Tennessee to work on. I've emailed everyone the schedule already. Some of you start tomorrow."

"Excuse me one second," Cooper interrupted. "If he's training everyone, when does he get a break?"

"Why does he need a break?" Royce whined. "Only humans need rest."

"He'll be kicking our asses without breaking a sweat all summer," Easton groaned and threw himself back against the table.

I cursed and all of the oxygen in my body left me in a rush. It didn't matter what the details were. They were going to suck. "Can we start right now? Because I can hardly contain my excitement. Do you see it in my face?"

Kessler rolled his golden eyes. "I'd like to take this opportunity to remind all of you that these two girls are strictly off-limits for dating." He took the time to glare at each and every one of the guys.

"Don't glare at me." Easton held his palms up. "I'm taken."

"I know you all know *why* we have this rule..." Kessler all but growled.

Yeah, we knew. Everyone knew. Salem's prophecy was Witchcraft 101. At our school, Edenburg, there was an entire course on what went down in Salem and the subsequent witch trials. It'd been over three hundred years, yet we treated it like last week's news. Our race was created after the fall of Eden, and there had never been a set of twins born within us until 1674. Until then, the demons had to struggle to get into our world. Since then, they walked through the Gaps. The original twins, as they were called now, had created the initial Gap. Long story short... hell hath no fury like a woman scorned.

Sadly, no one remembered the men who broke their hearts...only the ramifications.

When Kessler's twin nieces were born sixteen years ago, the Coven leaders laid down a race-wide law forbidding any and all romantic entanglements. No exceptions.

"Okay, that's enough for one day. Get going." Kessler dismissed everyone then turned to Cassandra and whispered.

I had questions. Lots of questions. But I needed to rein in the chaos inside me first. I turned and headed back toward the building to my first class of open house.

"Hey, Tennessee!"

I stopped and spun toward my name. The girl skipping toward me was one of my human friends I'd had most of my high school classes with. She had pale blonde hair she wore in wild waves from spending her mornings at the beach, and eyes that looked like Hershey's kisses. Her smile was friendly, although it'd gotten a little *friendlier* in the last few months.

"Hey, Ally."

Her smile widened, and she stopped a foot in front of me. "Hi, Tennessee. I've been looking for you all night."

*The night just started. Stop it. Be nice.* "Here I am."

"I texted you a few times... Maybe you didn't get them?"

*Crap.* I got them. I ignored them. Why? Who knew? "Sorry, it's been a crazy few days."

"It's okay!" She beamed and bounced up on her tippy toes. "Listen, my friends and I are going to Hidden Kingdom tomorrow, and I wanted to invite you to join us."

"Yes, he will," Easton said from out of nowhere. I hadn't seen or heard him walk up behind me, which wasn't like me at all. "He'd love to."

"You would?" Her brown eyes danced with excitement and her cheeks flushed.

*Fantastic.* If I said no now, I'd look like a real jerk. "Sure, I'd love to."

"Awesome! I'll text you in the morning, so you better answer." She winked and sauntered away. She completely ignored Easton's presence.

"You're welcome, my friend." Easton clapped me on the back.

"I didn't need you to step in," I snapped.

"Yes. You did. You're a walking ball of tension. You need some female attention." Easton mimicked her wink and swished his hips the way only an overly confident man could.

I cursed. I may have been tense, but women were not my answer. Especially not one I had no interest in romantically. But Easton won that round. I'd go, and I'd try my hardest to enjoy my free time. Because it might be my last chance to actually be a teenager for a while.

And—if I was completely honest with myself—I'd search every corner of the theme park until I found that little fairy.

*Seek the tool from thieving hands...*

# CHAPTER FOUR

Note to self: *When it's time to train Easton, make sure you leave a few marks. And if you can make him puke at least once, you get bonus points.*

Go to the theme park with some human girls, he said. It would be fun, he said. Yeah, well, he lied. Kessler had even allowed me to postpone my first training session when he found out I had plans with friends. What did that say about me? I should've told Ally no and went ahead with training.

Instead, I stood outside a store holding three purses while the girls took a shopping break. I could've gone inside with them. Ally practically begged me to, but I refused. There were so many people crammed into the store you couldn't take a step without running into a shelf, loose toddler, or a sweaty human. Sure, it was crowded outside, too, but at least the crying babies and screaming mothers weren't a foot away from me. They were like eight feet away. This part of the park was the quaint little French village, with cobblestone streets and fancy iron gates. Any minute now, Ally would find me, and the tedious conversation would commence.

I simply didn't have anything in common with them, so I didn't know how to interact. Maybe I didn't have anything in common with humans at all anymore. Wondering if Tyga was actually the secret father of Kylie Jenner's baby didn't make it onto my to-do list. I hated that I even knew their names. The Kardashians, that is, not my human friends. I sighed and leaned against the brick wall outside the shop, careful not to drop the three purses draped over my arms.

"The Emperor holds handbags now?" Cassandra's soft voice interrupted my inner anguish. "I'll have to update my tarot cards with this image."

Despite my foul mood, I laughed and turned to smile at my friend. "Save me?"

She cocked her head to the side, and her long red curls bounced. There was a wicked gleam in her emerald eyes, and I knew some serious sass was about to follow. She stepped around some tourists eyeing their park map and closed the distance between us. "Shall I break my ankle and fall over so you have to carry me home?"

I groaned and rolled my eyes. "So you heard."

"Did I ever." She giggled. "Did you know there's a debate going on about you?"

I stared out at the crowds passing by and the people trying to swim upstream in the traffic. The smell of French fries wafted by my face, and my stomach growled. *Maybe I can sneak over and get food while they're shopping?* "About what? This doesn't have to do with Royce calling me inhuman, does it?"

"No... I shouldn't tell you this, but family has to stick together, right?" She bit her bottom lip. When I just stared at her, she continued. "They're debating which of your eyes is hotter...the green one or the blue one."

My jaw dropped. Royce and Libby's comments from the last few days popped into memory with new light. "Seriously? That's weird, right?"

She chuckled and shrugged her pale, freckled shoulders. "I don't know, girls will be girls. I'm sure you'll hear the results of the vote once it's officially tallied."

"Lucky me." I knew by her smirk and the twitch of her eyebrow she wanted to harass me for it, so I took away her chance by changing the subject. "What brings you here today?"

"I hoped I'd have better luck with our thieving friend if I was alone." She leaned against the brick wall beside me. "You were right not to tell the others. Little pink wings is skittish. I followed her to the castle then lost her."

"Maybe she won't notice me if she's busy looking for you?"

"Possibly." She nodded. "Try charming her. You'll have to ditch these girls, though."

The door to my left swung open, and the four girls skipped back to my side like they'd been summoned. Not that I compared them to demons. They each had a new shopping bag in one hand and a bright colored drink in the other.

I sighed and glanced back over to Cassandra. "Gladly."

She laughed, gave me a fist bump, and backed away. "See ya later, Tenn," she yelled over her shoulder.

"What's her name again?" Ally asked from way, way too close to me. Her fruity perfume burned my nose.

"Cassandra."

"Isn't she too old to hang out with high school boys?" Ally's blonde friend asked. "As in, isn't it illegal?"

*Illegal?* How could being friends be...*oh. OH.* I scowled. "She's only thirty, and no. She's like my sister. She helped raise Cooper and me when we were little." Cassandra was one of my closest, dearest friends. Next in line of importance after Kessler and Cooper. Not having her in my life would be devastating. The idea of dating her actually made my stomach turn.

Ally's smile brightened. "Good to know. So, we're gonna get lunch next. Hungry?"

*Well there goes my escape plan. Wait...lunch? How is it*

*only lunch time?* Yeah, Easton was definitely going to pay. It was time for me to make my break. I had a tool to steal back from an elusive fairy.

With a feigned smile, I handed the girls back their handbags and stretched my arms. "Actually, no. You go ahead. I have to run an errand for Kessler. Maybe I'll catch back up with you later."

"Oh..." Ally's expression sank. "Okay. I'll text you after lunch."

Guilt tugged at me, but I pushed it down. I'd spent five hours with her already. I knew what she wanted from me... I just didn't feel anything for her. *I'm supposed to feel something, aren't I?*

"Enjoy lunch," I said.

If they had more to say, I didn't hear it. Now that I had my getaway, I wouldn't risk losing it because I was a nice guy. I turned and beelined past the fountain. Without slowing my pace, I headed up the cobblestone pathway to the castle in the back of the park. Witches had been guarding it for almost five hundred years, both from humans and *for* humans. Adding it to the Hidden Kingdom theme park was part of the cover-up of The Great Loss.

I walked around the staggering line of little girls waiting to be dolled up like princesses at the boutique, and slid through the horde of tourists watching the show on the main stage. The wait for the Royal Table lunch had to be two hours long based on the human chain down the pathway. None of these were of interest to me. No, I needed the back side of the castle where the hidden staircase winded up the tower and provided an excellent vantage point for finding fairies.

I was halfway up when I spotted her tucked away in a castle window and brushing her fiery hair. I froze mid step to avoid spooking her. If I hadn't known what she looked like, I might've missed her. She couldn't have been more than two feet tall, and her little transparent pink wings were definitely larger than her body. Truth was, I'd never actually seen a real, living fairy before. Apparently they rarely ventured out of their realm anymore, except for this one who wouldn't leave ours.

*Okay, little miss, here I come.* I took three steps, and her head snapped to me. Her big eyes widened. We stared at each other for a long moment, neither of us moving an inch until a pigeon landed on the windowsill and she took off like a bat out of hell. I raced down the steps, running parallel to her path. She looked over her shoulder and then took a sharp right and flew toward the forested area behind the castle. Without slowing my pace, I leapt over the rail and slid down the pitched roof that covered the pedestrian pathway. The shingles rattled under my weight, but I glided over them like it was a Slip 'N Slide. Part of me wondered what the humans below me heard, but I pushed the thought away.

Just before I reached the edge, I jumped up, caught the thick branch of an oak tree, and swung myself around it like a gymnast on uneven bars to keep my momentum going. When my feet hit the dirt, I rolled into a somersault and pushed off the ground into a sprint. My little fairy friend had the upper hand with her wings, but I had magical powers on my side. I summoned gusts of wind and slammed them into her head-on. Her wings fluttered and struggled to fly against the wind, slowing her pace significantly. I pushed my powers full throttle, thankful for the cloak of trees to hide my glowing skin.

I was three feet from her when she pulled her wings in and rolled to the left. She disappeared between the trees. I swung around the base of a tree and raced after her with my arm outstretched. Her translucent pink wings brushed over my fingertips like mist. I tried to grab hold, but they didn't appear to be solid in form. She crossed over the pathway of human tourists completely unseen, like she had some type of glamour to hide her.

For years I'd lectured and chastised my fellow Cards for reckless behavior around Sapiens. I told them to not use their magic in the open. I told them not to endanger the humans in any way. I was about to become a hypocrite. If she got into the main part of the park, I'd lose her, and I didn't know when or if I'd find her again. Now that she definitely knew we were after her, would she finally return to her realm? I couldn't risk it. She'd stolen the tool we needed. Without it, our quest couldn't be completed. Something told me this quest coinciding with the twins' arrival wasn't a coincidence. We'd need this tool to close the Gap.

*Desperate times, desperate measures.* I said a silent prayer to the Goddess to protect the Sapiens and then unleashed my power into the ground. The pathway trembled, and humans dropped to the floor. A hundred screaming voices pierced my ears. Bricks popped loose of the pathway, and without hesitating, I summoned enough wind to turn them into projectiles aimed right at my little fairy friend. She squealed and dodged a few, but one caught her in the gut and knocked her to the ground. I jumped over the rail and skipped over the scrambling humans, but she was too fast. She shook her wings once then flew right through an open door and inside one of the attractions.

I cursed and slid to a stop... *Wait.* I glanced up to the sign and sighed. THE HAUNTED PALACE. There was only one place in the entire theme park where magic could be hidden...perhaps my luck had just improved.

I dropped the earthquake and sprinted through the front doors of the ride. People lined the hallways, waiting patiently for their turn. I heard them yell out in protest while I ran by, skipping the line without hesitation. The fairy didn't look back once inside. She zipped right through like she hung out there often and slipped past the ride attendants. Not a single person noticed her disappear around the corner except me.

I jumped over the queue and ran up the exit lane to where the attendants loaded tourists into their designated buggy. An elderly couple took their time moving up to their buggy, leaving three empty ones up ahead. I sprinted forward and slid into one of the empty, clamshell-like buggies. The ride jerked into motion, and the bar lowered closer to my lap.

The ride took the cars on a journey through a haunted estate where ghosts jumped out and tried to scare people. After dealing with real evil spirits, the holographic ones were a picnic. The ride moved through a dimly lit hallway where doors lined each side. Each wooden doorframe was enhanced with a spooky effect.

An icy chill brushed over my back. I looked left and right, up and down, and then repeated the process. Every flash of light caught my attention. The ride crawled around a dark corner before stopping completely.

"Attention guests, please remain in your ghost buggy."

"Fat chance," I mumbled to myself.

The room was only lit by a black light. In the center, a crystal ball glistened with swirling colors while neon-painted objects floated above my head. Before the ride started moving again, I slid out of my buggy and onto solid ground. I closed my eyes and listened. Fake musical instruments chimed, a woman's voice echoed all around me, and something clapped softly.

*Wait... I wonder.* I bounced to the balls of my feet, ready to take off, then I summoned the cold air from the air conditioner and pushed it through the room. The clapping noise got louder and faster, almost frantic. I blocked out all the other noises and focused on the flapping. It was up in the corner to my left. I moved closer until it sounded right above me, and I crouched down, still on the balls of my feet. The ride screeched behind me and immediately began moving through the room. I held my left palm up and willed my arm to light up, then slammed the glow up to the ceiling.

My little fairy friend shrieked and took off. This time I was ready and chased her out of the dark room, hot on her heels. Her wings fluttered so fast all I saw were the fiery red strands of her hair flying in the air. I dodged tourist-filled buggies and leapt over props while racing after her. I chased her through the Grand Parlor room full of holographic dancing ghosts, but when we turned the corner, she hit the sheer net they projected ghosts onto and dropped to the ground...right in the middle of the mock cemetery.

I moved toward where she fell when a ghost popped up in front of my face. I jumped to the left and met another one. I took a step to the right except this time the hologram followed me. *Relax, Tennessee. It's just a special effect.* The fairy scrambled to her feet, but when I tried to get closer, the ghost grabbed my arm and pulled. I gasped and spun around. Its grip stung like ice against my skin. *Oh hell... Here?* This wasn't a hologram; it was a real ghost and one pissed off enough to come out in the middle of the day and approach me. They weren't supposed to be inside the ride at all.

"What are you doing in here?" I asked the ghost while my brain tried to catch up.

Part of me wondered what Kessler would say about this. The other part of me belatedly realized none of the ghosts in the cemetery room were holographic. All of them glowered at me. I reached to my hip for my sword and remembered I'd left it at home, because the Sapiens would've been weirded out by it. My next few moves had to be done fast. I stretched my right hand out wide without moving my arm and called for the dagger tucked inside my boot. The second the handle hit my palm, a calming power tingled up my arm, and I slashed my weapon through the ghost holding me.

In a flash, two dozen ghosts swarmed with their icy hands outstretched. They couldn't physically harm the Sapiens, but the Goddess's blood in my veins made them capable of killing a witch.

*Yeah, well, not today psycho.* I waited until they were a foot in front of me and then jumped straight up in the air and flipped over backwards. As I landed, I brought my dagger down in an arch and sliced through them in a blur of light. I spun, ducked, and slashed in a line. Styrofoam gravestones wavered as I jumped over them like a track star. Another horde of ghosts popped up in my path. I slid, dragging my dagger through as many as I could. When I fell to my knees, I summoned all of my energy and then pushed it out in one massive sonic boom. All of the ghosts disintegrated in an instant.

The lights in the ride flickered twice before drenching the humans in darkness. Screams and shrieks of terror filled the fake cemetery, their buggies locked in place. But I couldn't waste any time on them. I had to find my fairy friend. I tucked my dagger back into my boot and moved through the plastic props and projection screens by the light coming off my skin. Despite the chaos from the humans, I picked up on one sound that wasn't like the others. It was high-pitched, but soft...and it was crying.

I followed the whimper into the back corner of the room. It took me a second to spot her huddled inside a Styrofoam mausoleum. She had her arms wrapped tightly around her knees, and her wings draped her like cocoon. I froze in my tracks, completely caught off guard by the sight. For the first time in minutes, I felt the pounding of my heart in my chest as my body tried to calm itself.

I crept closer to her hiding spot, crouched in a low squat so I wouldn't scare her. Up close, with the light coming off my body, her skin was pale and covered in goose bumps. *What now?* I hadn't expected her to be scared of me, or anything. I tried to use my softest voice. "Hey there."

She jumped and scurried farther into the corner. "No, no, no. No. Go."

I raised my palms in the air in surrender. "I'm not going to hurt you."

"I'm always hurt," she said with a trembling voice that sounded like wind chimes.

*Be charming. That's what Cassandra told me.* "You don't cause any trouble."

She shook her head and sobbed. "Please, no trouble. Don't chase me. Scare me."

"I didn't mean to scare you. I only chased you because you have something I need."

Her eyes widened, and I noticed for the first time they were a bright lavender. "I don't have anything at all!" she wailed.

Okay, I needed a new angle. *Be charming.* I took a deep breath. "Hey, hey, it's okay. What's your name?"

She looked up at me and sniffed. "Saffie."

I smiled. "I'm Tennessee. It's nice to meet you."

Tears of shimmering silver streaked down her angled cheeks. "You nice to me? No one is nice to Saffie. I have no friends."

My heart sank, and for more than one reason. For one, I was prepared to kill this little fairy in order to get the tool.

I hadn't considered a different option. The other Cards wouldn't have hesitated either. But also...how many times in all these years had I seen her and completely ignored her?

"Well, we can be friends," I said.

"Really?" Her eyes lit up for a second before she sank back into suspicion. "What do you want from me to be your friend?"

For some strange reason, a surge of protectiveness soared through me. Who had hurt her and why? Now more than ever, I wanted to know why she was here, but it wasn't the time for that.

I shook my head. "Real friendship doesn't cost anything."

"You promise?"

"How do you make promises in your realm?"

"You can't break that." She stared at me for a long minute or two, and I knew she was trying to decide whether or not to trust me. Finally, she crawled to the edge and held up her little hand with her pinky finger out. "Like this..."

*Pinky promise?* Somewhere in the back of my mind, I knew this might be a horrible, dangerous idea, but I ignored it. I held my pinky out to hers and stopped myself from jumping when her cold finger wrapped around mine. Her skin was softer than silk.

"I promise...?" I started.

"On a bed of rose thorns."

*Yeah, might be bad indeed.* Too late to back out. "I promise on a bed of rose thorns we are friends, Saffie."

"I promise on a sea of spider lilies we are friends... Tennessee." She looked up at me with the biggest smile I'd ever seen, and it made me feel a little better about the oath I'd just made. "Now, friend, tell me why you're chasing me? Please?"

I swallowed down my unease. "Well, the other night the demon threw something into the Gap, but I saw you catch it. Problem is, I need that object."

She frowned. "What for?"

"To help us close the Gaps forever."

"Like it used to be?"

*How old are you, Saffie?* 'It used to be' meant prior to Salem 1692. She'd have to be over three hundred years old to remember. One day soon I would have to figure her out.

I nodded. "Yes, like before Salem."

She nodded and reached down into the little dress she had on. "You mean this?"

The object she held out was small, maybe an inch long and shimmery, but without proper lighting, I couldn't tell. I knew it was the object the demon threw though.

"Yes," I said.

"It's pretty." She sighed and looked down at the object in her palm. "You want me to give it to you?"

"I really need it to save people."

"It keeps Saffie safe. It scares monsters away. I'm always so scared until I found this."

*Note to self: talk to Cassandra about fairies and Saffie.* "What if I gave you something else to keep you safe and scare away monsters?"

She sat up straight and nodded. "Please? I don't like being scared."

"Yeah, of course." A crazy idea popped into my head, one I might regret later. Then again, I might be thankful later too.

When I'd first moved in with Kessler he made me a ring entirely out of white quartz. He'd said the stone had calming powers, and it tricked demons and evil spirits into thinking the wearer was a human.

I reached down to my left pinky finger, the only one it still fit, and slid it off. "This is a..."

"Stardust quartz ring!" She squealed and snatched it out of my palm. Her face split into a wide grin, her lavender eyes sparkling. "Thank you, my friend, Tennessee!"

"You know what it is?"

She nodded and slid the ring onto her thumb. The quartz warped and shifted to fit her finger. "It has fairy magic. Thank you. I will be not scared now."

I smiled. "You're welcome."

"Here, you can save people now." She held her hand

out and dropped the stolen item into my palm. "Next time you see me, you can say hi, not chase me. Okay?"

I chuckled. "Deal. Thank you, Saffie. I have to bring this to my father now, but will you be okay here?"

She beamed up at me. "I have hiding spots everywhere. Yes."

I nodded and stood to my full height, gripping the tool in my hand. The second it hit my skin, I knew what it was, without having to see it. *You gotta call Kessler.* "See you later, Saffie."

"Bye bye, Tennessee!" In the blink of an eye, she was gone.

I stood there for a second shaking my head at what had transpired until it hit me. *I have the tool. I did it.*

Then reality crashed back around me. The ride was still broken down, in the dark with people freaking out. I raced across the cemetery to where an emergency exit was tucked into the back corner, and then slipped out. The sunlight stung my eyes and the heat choked me. But I had the tool.

I pulled my phone out and dialed Kessler. "Emergency meeting now. I have the tool... It's a pendulum."

# CHAPTER FIVE

Twenty-five minutes later, I walked through the front door of my ranch style house and found my entire crew piled on the two tan leather couches in my living room, staring at the foyer. I frowned and looked around. They were literally piled on top of each other. Some of the smaller girls sat on top of others' laps. Peabo and Atley were perched on the back of one sofa. Cooper half cheeked it on one armrest. Kessler sat on the edge of one sofa, with Cassandra squeezed in next to him beside Easton. Even Braison's dog Albert was curled up under his owner's legs on the carpet. Part of me wondered why no one had at least brought in a chair from the dining room ten feet away or a stool from the kitchen counter two feet away.

I took a moment to compose myself, to sound calm and

confident and not in the least bit concerned. Thirteen Cards and two warriors-in-training sat in silence...waiting. The hectic energy in the room sizzled my senses and made the hairs on my arms stand straight up. They were nervous, anxious, and a little bit excited. With every step I took into the room, they sat up straighter and their eyes sharpened.

Kessler stood and waved me forward. "Let's get right to it. Son, show everyone, please."

The crystal warmed in my palm, like it knew it was being spoken about. I hadn't put it down once since Saffie gave it to me, not even into my pocket. During the entire walk out of the park and drive home, the tool was wrapped tightly in my grip. I'd peeked at it a few times, unable to stop myself. The crystal shimmered a soft blueish-purple, but in the sunlight, it morphed into a rosy pink. I might've missed a few green lights from staring at it. I took a deep breath and uncurled my fingers, revealing a blueish crystal in the center of my palm.

"It really is a pendulum..." Cassandra whispered. Her emerald green eyes were wide and her mouth hung open. She held her red-freckled hand out, and her blue nail polish was chipped, like she'd started biting her nails again. "May I?"

I stepped forward and lowered my palm for her to take it. Her pale fingers were a stark contrast to my tan skin. Everyone else leaned forward to watch and gauge her reaction. She scooched to the edge of the couch and held the crystal up to her face. I shifted my weight around, waiting for her to relieve me and take over control of this situation. She had to have the answers; she always did. Fifteen pairs of eyes on me made me twitch, but Cassandra didn't seem to notice.

"I don't get it," Easton said and leaned over Cassandra's left shoulder to look. His trademark wild grin was nowhere in sight. Even his light blue eyes looked a little darker. He scratched the blond scruff on his jaw. A serious Easton would take some getting used to. "How is a pendulum going to help us?"

"I'm not sure," I admitted.

The central air conditioner kicked on, and a cold breeze brushed over my back. The sweat on my spine made my T-shirt cling to my skin. I rolled my neck and tried to release the tension in my muscles. This was only one piece of the quest, so I couldn't let myself get too excited or relieved. I looked to Cassandra, waiting along with everyone else.

Royce slid Willow off his lap and jumped over to the empty seat next to Cassandra. He leaned over her shoulder and frowned. "Henley has like a thousand pendulums hanging in her room. Why did we need *this* one?"

I looked over and smiled at the sight of her dark attire in front of the white wall. The only part of Henley not covered in something black were her porcelain face and hands. Even her lips were painted black today.

She scoffed. "When did we start questioning the Goddess?"

"I question everything." The tan leather couch creaked as Libby leaned around Chutney and winked in Henley's direction.

Cooper walked over and crouched in front of Easton to look at the crystal hanging from a dark gold chain. "How did you get it from the fairy?"

All at once, questions fired at me one after another about the fairy. I wasn't even sure who asked which.

"Yeah, did you kill her?"

"I bet she's mean."

"How much of a fight did she put up?"

"Did she have any other information?"

I bit my lip and hesitated to answer. Telling them the whole truth felt like stripping down naked in front of them and doing the funky chicken. Although, I didn't know *why* it made me so vulnerable. I'd made an unexpected friend... No big deal. *Right?* I couldn't lie and say I'd killed her for obvious reasons, but did I admit she was actually nice and just scared? That seemed like a betrayal of her trust. I didn't even want to tell them her name.

"I didn't hurt her, and she didn't attack me. We made a trade. There's definitely more to her story than we know, and when we're done with this quest, Kessler, I'd like to find out."

My father took a long hard look at me before nodding. He'd been standing silently behind the couch, watching over everyone's shoulders. His arms were crossed over his chest, the telltale sign he was worried. "Okay."

I knew by the set of his jaw and the intensity in his golden eyes he had more to say on the situation, but he seemed to accept it for now. He knew I liked to keep things private. He'd ask me later; we both knew it.

I nodded and then turned my attention back to Cassandra. "Well, what do you think, George?"

Her lips curled into a smirk at her nickname. "I think we should try using it like we would any pendulum." She moved to the ground and sat cross-legged on the white carpet.

Everyone moved into a circle around her, careful to leave her space but eager to see what happened. We watched in silence. Sunlight poured in from the nearby French windows, making the crystal turn a rosy pink wherever the light hit. Cassandra placed her right elbow on the glass table and held her hand out in front of her. The crystal looked like a chunk of the sky hanging from a chain. She waited until the crystal stopped swaying and hung straight down, then she closed her eyes and breathed. We knew not to speak or it would interrupt the energy connection. My pulse pounded in my veins with anticipation. *Please let this work.*

With the chain loosely gripped between her thumb and middle fingertip, she spoke softly. "Show me yes."

Nothing happened. I cursed under my breath. Everyone took a step back at the same time. Sometimes at first use, the pendulum needed space. When she asked it to *show* her, it meant the crystal was supposed to swing in a direction signifying yes. Once it showed yes, she'd ask it to show no, I don't know, and I don't want to answer. It was really cool to watch the crystal respond on its own. Sometimes the most basic magic was the most exciting to witness.

"Show me *yes*," she repeated.

Again, nothing.

She narrowed her eyes. "Show me *no.*"

Nothing.

"It's not connecting to me," Cassandra said with more frustration in her voice than I'd ever heard. She sighed and rubbed her face with her free hand.

"Want me to try?" Easton asked with bright eyes and his hand up in the air. He wagged his eyebrows playfully. *Serious Easton hadn't lasted long.*

Cassandra shook her head. Slowly, her gaze moved to meet mine, and my chest filled with dread. "Sometimes powerful tools like this can only be used by the witch who claimed it. Tennessee, we need you to try."

I sighed, but wasn't surprised. Part of me expected it, but none of me was excited about it. Sure, the magic part was fun, but the pressure on me wasn't. I wiped my palms on my black jeans and prayed my fingers wouldn't betray my confidence. I moved to sit on the carpet beside Cassandra and took the pendulum she held out. The crystal immediately warmed against my palm. My pulse skipped a beat. When I took the chain between my two fingers like Cassandra had, an electric shock shot up my arm. I gasped and the crystal bobbed in the air. *Whoa. Okay, maybe it does like me.*

Cassandra inhaled. "I knew it. Keep going."

The rest of my gang leaned closer with encouraging smiles. A few of them even gave me a thumbs-up. Kessler moved into my line of view, one hand pulling on his bottom lip. He stared at the pendulum for a second then met my gaze and nodded. I swallowed nervously and followed Cassandra's lead, placing my right elbow on the glass table and holding my hand out. The crystal swayed for a few seconds before it settled in straight. I knew how to use a pendulum; it was pretty much Witchcraft 101, but I also knew with total certainty this was not a normal crystal.

"Show me yes," I said.

The crystal didn't swing or spin, but I thought I saw it jolt. My lips twitched, but I suppressed a smile. *Okay, focus. You can do this.*

I licked my lips and channeled my energy into the pendulum. "Show me yes."

Again, the stone remained motionless. Except this time a purple mist spilled out from the crystal and swirled through the air around the stone. *It's working.*

I tried to focus, but everyone was whispering around me and it was distracting. "Can you guys stop talking?"

"Um...Tennessee...no one is talking..." Cooper said with a soft, gentle voice.

I frowned and looked around.

Everyone eyed me with alarmed expressions on their faces.

"None of you were whispering just now? None of you hear it?" I asked.

"No, we can't. But you can." Cassandra pursed her lips and tapped her chin with her finger. "I was right. It's only wanting to answer to you. You are the chosen one for this."

"Then why isn't it working?" Royce asked. The leather couch creaked like he'd moved closer.

"I think he needs to try it *alone.* Tenn, go into the other room and shut the door. Then try it."

Of course, I had to do it alone. Lately almost everything I did either placed me at project leader or riding solo. Although if I had to be the one to do it, I'd rather not have everyone watching. I stood and walked to the doorway of Kessler's office where I'd have privacy.

I paused with my hand on the door and my eyes on the

pendulum. "Is there something specific you want me to ask it?"

"We need to know if it will help close the Gap." Cassandra tapped her fingers on the glass table. "But just see if it responds to you first. We can formulate what we want to ask later."

I nodded. *Just see if it works.* No big deal. Without another word, I shut the French door and pulled the white drapes over the glass. The beach wood floors creaked as I crossed the room and sat in the cozy brown chair beside the window. There was a small round glass-topped end table in front of me.

*Breathe.* I placed my elbow on the glass like I had in the living room and let the pendulum swing from my fingertips. Once it stopped, I focused my energy through the gold chain and into the crystal. "Show me *yes.*"

Instantly, the pendulum swung in a straight line away from my body and back. I inhaled in surprise. A chuckle slipped out of my mouth. *Cool.* Now that I was alone, I let myself enjoy the moment. With a smile, I refocused my energy. "Show me *no.*"

The pendulum swung back toward my body but stopped abruptly in the middle like I'd touched it. Then it switched direction and swung left to right, right to left. My heart skipped a beat before jumping into overdrive.

I licked my lips. *Okay, stay cool, stay cool.* "Show me I don't know."

Again, the pendulum stopped itself mid swing. This time it moved in a wide clockwise circle. *Amazing.* Pendulums were a popular witch tool, but I'd never seen one respond quite so passionately.

My heart pounded in my chest. Only one more response question left. "Show me I don't want to answer."

Even though I knew it would happen, it still made me gasp when the pendulum switched direction and swung in a counterclockwise circle.

I exhaled. The pendulum worked for me. *Time to test it out.* "Stop."

The pendulum ceased motion and hung straight down like it wasn't a magical tool. The sunlight streaming through the window turned half of the crystal a rosy pink.

*Focus, Tennessee.* "Is this pendulum the tool from the prophecy?"

The crystal swung away from me and back. *Yes.*

"Stop. Am I the chosen witch for this tool?"

It repeated the same swing.

"Stop. Will this pendulum answer to any other witch?"

The crystal soared from left to right. *No.*

"Stop. Do I need this tool to close the Gap in Salem?"

It switched motion back to signify yes. I nodded. I had suspected as much. I knew Cassandra said to test if it worked and then we'd figure out what to ask it, but there was one thing I needed to know. I took a deep breath and wiped the sweat beading on my forehead with my free hand. "Stop. Will I have a big role in closing the Gap in Salem?"

If possible, the pendulum swung faster and wider than it had before. Or perhaps it was my imagination? Either way, it told me the answer I secretly didn't want to accept. Now I'd have to. When it came time to close the main Gap, the *original* Gap in Salem, I would play a major role. *Yippy.*

I gripped the crystal in my palm and made my way back to where my Coven waited. When I opened the door, fifteen pairs of anxious eyes snapped to attention. Any whispered conversations cut off. No one had moved from the spots they'd been in before. They still piled on top of the couches like a litter of puppies.

Cassandra jumped to her feet. Her green eyes widened. "Did it work?"

"Yes."

They cheered and high-fived each other. Cassandra rubbed her palms together, already working on the next step in her head. Kessler nodded and finally uncrossed his arms from his chest, pacing behind the couches.

I cleared my throat. "I confirmed it is the tool from the prophecy. It won't answer to anyone else but me...and it is needed for closing the Gap."

Silence.

No one was surprised or relieved. A few of the younger girls exchanged cagey looks. Peabo and Atley, our non-Card warriors-in-training, frowned and scratched their heads like they were confused. But everyone else sobered into battle mode. I recognized the sharp looks in their eyes. All the years we'd been waiting and training, and now it was finally here. Playtime was over.

I looked to my father for directions since the next step would come from him. "What do you want to do now?"

"Well..." Kessler sighed and scratched the back of his head. He finally stopped pacing and looked around the room. His eyes sparkled in the beam of sunlight, but they were distant, like his thoughts were miles away. "You've got a training session with Larissa, Paulina, Henley, and Lily."

"Wait, what?" Henley frowned and stood. She raised her black ring-clad hands in the air. "Don't we have more important things to do?"

Kessler arched one blond eyebrow at her. "Than getting you ready for the fight of your life? No. We have to continue as planned."

Cassandra walked over and wrapped her arm around Henley's shoulders. "He's right. Go train. I need to be alone to process all of this. Besides, exercising his body will help Tennessee think clearly."

*Think clearly. Right.* I didn't know if my brain was capable of thinking *clearly* right now, but I sure as hell could use the exercise. In fact, I needed to shut my brain off for a while. Weapons and magic were the perfect solution.

I shoved the pendulum into the front pocket of my jeans. "All right, ladies, you heard them. Let's go kick your asses."

# CHAPTER SIX

I slid and dropped down to one knee to dodge Larissa's attack. Sand splattered her like a tidal wave. Her long wooden bat missed my forehead by an inch, brushing over my sweaty hair instead. I spun and swung my bat, taking her long legs out from underneath her. She dropped to the sand with a heavy thud and a curse. Lily raised her bat and charged with a battle cry. Her black hair was matted to her forehead with sweat. I jumped to my feet and raced toward her, but instead of meeting her with my weapon, I ducked and flipped her over my back.

White light flashed in my peripheral vision. I turned just in time to watch Paulina soar through the air and land ten feet away with white magic flickering around her body. Sand exploded around her like a bomb went off. To my left, Henley stood with her bat like it was a giant wand.

White magic swirled around the wooden weapon like a snake.

I inhaled the salty ocean air and tried to keep my voice calm. Patience was key for teaching, but my frustration with her stubbornness was at its limits. "Henley, for the eight hundredth time, no magic."

Henley groaned and rolled her sapphire blue eyes. She looked rough. Her dark eyeshadow was smudged across her face, and her black lipstick smeared over her chin. The hoop piercing she always wore on her bottom lip was missing, though I hoped she'd taken if off before we started. Behind her, the moon twinkled a little brighter, responding to her energy.

"We're witches!" she said.

I shook my head and put my hands on my hips. I counted to five while the waves crashed ashore to my right. We'd been out here on the beach for three hours training, yet I couldn't get them to stop using their magical powers. My job wasn't to harness their mystical talents. I needed to get their combat skills up to par. Once the twins arrived, the demon attacks would increase. Kessler had told us repeatedly. I had to make sure my Coven knew what to do.

"We've gone over this, Henley. Cassandra is working with everyone's magic. My job is to test your battle skills," I said.

"I don't have battle skills." She crossed her arms over her chest. The constellation tattoos on her wrists reminded me that she'd only get harder to rein in as sunset approached.

"Evidently."

I ignored the sand she kicked in my direction.

"Tennessee, c'mon, we've been out here forever." Paulina whined. Her soft Spanish accent rolled like the waves and sounded just as pretty. Her long body still lay sprawled on the sand from Henley's spell. She looked like a caramel-colored starfish that'd been washed ashore. Her long dark curls dripped with sweat. I didn't like how hard she breathed. "The sun is done."

"Actually, I'm fine." Lily smirked and adjusted her black ponytail. Her lavender eyes perfectly matched the colors of the sunset behind her. The letters XIX stood out on her olive skin. Her tarot Mark was the Sun, and like it, her energy level seemed endless. "Give Moonchild a break. You know she can't help herself this close to dark."

Henley, aka Moonchild, aka The Moon, sighed dramatically and dropped to the ground. "Someone gets me." Her XVIII Mark took up the entire width of her porcelain skin, although it was almost completely hidden under her black fishnet shirt.

"No, but really. Sunset is rapidly approaching." Paulina still hadn't moved except to wipe the sweat from her cleavage. "I'm no dainty thing, but we've been busting our asses for hours now."

"She has a point, Tenn." Larissa shrugged. In the

fading sun, her mocha skin looked almost mahogany. The thick faux-hawk braid she'd done during warm-up stayed perfectly intact, and I made a mental note to have her teach me how to do my own. "We don't have your energy."

Henley walked up to me with narrowed eyes. "Listen here, Emperor. What do we need to do to end this training session?"

I sighed. Had I trained them too hard? Maybe Kessler hadn't intended on such a long session. I was proud of them though. For hours they gave me their best effort. Perhaps I needed to cut them some slack on their first training session.

I rubbed my face with my palms, and the sand stuck to my hands irritated my skin. "Okay. We can call it a night."

"Thank the Goddess," Henley sang with a bright, black-smeared smile. She turned and headed to the ice chest I'd brought.

Larissa pulled Paulina to her feet and helped brush some of the sand off of her. Lily bumped my arm with her shoulder and waved for me to follow. I walked over and sat on the sand beside the four of them. For witches who focused on elemental magic, they really gave combat their all. They had raw talent we'd just never harnessed before, but I had a good feeling they'd progress quickly after a summer with me.

Because that's what Kessler had planned for my entire summer...training my fellow Cards. I got it, I really did. It was just going to be a lot of work. The girls needed to work on their instincts and how to fight without their magic. The guys needed to work on their skill level and stamina. I had to deliver both...*and* figure out the rest of the prophecy.

Anxiety rippled through me like an electric shock. My stomach turned and my chest got tight. *Seek the tool from thieving hands. First ally with those between the lands. To mend the bond between them all, listen for the vengeful Fallen's call.* I sighed. I'd accomplished the first task and retrieved the stolen tool. The bond between them all sounded like the Gap. The pendulum told me the tool was involved, so it was possible. But the other two lines written on Cassandra's arm were gibberish to me.

A hand landed on my forearm. "Tennessee?"

I jumped and found Henley's pale fingers on my skin. "Yeah?"

"Welcome back." She winked and removed her hand. "Where'd you go?"

*Ah, I spaced out again.* My cheeks warmed. "Sorry. I was thinking about the prophecy."

"Have you tried using the pendulum again?" Larissa met my gaze with eager hazel-green eyes. She uncapped a bottle of water and drank.

I shook my head. "No, I've been here with you guys."

Paulina cocked her head to the side. Sand was caked into her hair. "Do you know what the next line of prophecy means?"

"No."

"So, you don't know where to go next?" Lily asked.

I shook my head. I was as clueless and lost as everyone else, but I needed to not show it.

"Have the pendulum show you."

I frowned and looked to my right at Henley. "Have it show me?"

Henley blinked and met each one of our gazes. She shrugged and ran her black fingernailed hands through her shoulder-length black hair. "Pendulums are great for finding lost things. No reason it can't help with this."

I opened my mouth to speak then shut it. What had Royce said earlier? Something about Henley having hundreds of pendulums at home... Maybe I had room to learn from her. Crystal magic *was* Henley's preference.

I cleared my throat. "How does that work? It can't answer in full sentences."

"Crystals sense energy and magic..." She pursed her lips, her gaze off in the distance.

"What are you thinking?" I leaned forward to try and regain her attention. If she had any ideas how to help, I wanted to hear them. I may have had to do it alone, but it didn't mean I had to come up with the plan by myself.

She sighed. "Well, it may not work...but...maybe ask it if it detects any black energy. If it says yes, you can then use the pendulum like a compass. I've tried it before with my pendulums and it works."

My jaw dropped. *Like a compass.* I'd never thought of that. A flutter of hope and excitement wiggled in my chest. "How?" I needed to know *everything. Note to self: brush up on your basic magic skills asap.*

"Try saying, 'show me' or 'follow the trail.' Something like that."

All at once, my senses tingled, like I'd been plugged into an electrical socket. Henley had a great idea, and I wanted to try it. I pulled the pendulum out of my pocket and rolled the crystal between my fingertips. "Okay. I'll try it now. Thanks."

"You're welcome." Henley smiled and stood. "That's our cue, ladies. Let's leave The Emperor to his duty."

Lily stood but she eyed me warily. "If you're going to follow dark energy, we need to be nearby."

Paulina and Larissa exchanged nervous glances before getting to their feet.

"Fair point." I nodded and stared at the crystal. "Why don't you drive a mile or so away and park. If I need you, or if I find anything, I'll call you. In the meantime, you can call Cassandra and let her know what I'm trying."

All four girls nodded, wished me luck, then disappeared out of sight. I sat there in the warm, white powdery sand watching the sun set on the Gulf of Mexico. The breeze had dropped the temperature to a refreshingly cool feel, and it chilled the sweat rolling off my skin. Part of me considered taking my boots off and dumping the buckets of sand out, but I was too busy enjoying the view. The salty air and rolling waves chipped away the tension in my body.

After a few minutes, I propped my elbow on my knee and let the pendulum align itself. When it was still, I asked, "Do you know where I'm supposed to go next?"

The pendulum swung left to right. *Yes.* I stopped it with my free hand and considered my next question. I needed to word it right. "Can you show me where to go next?"

To my relief, it responded with a resounding *yes.*

I stopped the crystal and got to my feet.

That flutter of excitement returned. "Am I in the right spot now?"

It swung left and right again. *Of course not.*

I wrapped my hand around the pendulum and walked to my car. Once inside my Jeep, I backed out of my parking spot and held up the pendulum. "Please, show me where to go."

Just as Henley had said, the pendulum swung in the direction toward the main road. I followed its path until it switched direction and swung to the left. Fortunately, there was no one on the road in this secluded area, so I drove about fifteen miles per hour so I could watch the crystal and still drive safe. After about a mile of driving in the same direction without the pendulum changing, I wondered if it was working at all. I'd left the soft top of my Wrangler at home, so without any windows to block the wind, perhaps my connection to the stone had weakened. I sighed and rolled the Jeep to a stop at a stop sign. There was no one behind me, so I closed my eyes and tried to think. Did I call Henley and ask if I'd done it wrong? Out of the entire Coven, she had the most experience with pendulums. I was just about to pull out my cell phone when a shock zapped my fingers and tingled up my arm. I opened my eyes and found the pendulum swinging left to right.

*Holy crap. It worked.* I sat forward in my seat. My pulse skyrocketed. The crystal swung a little farther to the left than to the right.

"Okay, left it is." *Left on Ocean Drive.* I had no idea where we were headed, but after I turned left, the pendulum switched motion to lead me straight. My brain began hypothesizing of where it might be leading me, trying to predict where I'd turn next. The fact that it was working had me pumped. I couldn't wait to see what was next.

Four blocks down, another bolt of energy soared through my fingers. On reflex, I tensed. The pendulum flew to the right so wide it was almost parallel to the ground. I slammed on the breaks and made a seriously illegal right turn from the left lane. Horns blared and I didn't like how close those screeching tires sounded.

I cursed and chastised myself for not paying attention to the road. I hadn't even seen the other cars. My pulse raced through my veins. "Sorry!" I waved my free hand and yelled out to whoever I just cut off. I had no windows, so I figured they heard or saw it.

Part of me knew I needed to call Cassandra, but the other part of me wanted to follow the lead first. *Guess which part of me is about to win.*

I followed the pendulum's directions around three more turns until it led me to a one-way street, demanding I go down the wrong way. Option one: drive illegally and possibly get in an accident and hurt people. Option two: take the rest of it on foot in this impossible heat. I idled in indecision longer than I'd admit to anyone out loud before I parked my Jeep and got out.

Driving a soft top Wrangler meant there was no adjusting to temperature when you got in or out of the car. It was the same on both sides. This was both a perk and a con. Although now that I was walking and didn't have the rushing breeze, the heat settled on me like a hot, wet towel. Sweat trickled from my neck down to my back. I desperately wanted to tie my hair up to get some relief, but I refused to put the pendulum down and risk losing the connection.

"All right, let's do this." I held the pendulum up and took a deep breath. "Show me the way."

It swung back and forth, telling me to walk straight. I wasn't sure what the pendulum was following, but maybe it was dark magic like Henley mentioned. It seemed to have an end point in mind. Or at least I hoped so. I wasn't paying any attention to where I was, only where it led me.

The sun had officially set. All around me street lights came to life and shimmered their golden glow onto the ground. The air was hot and sticky, but at least the humidity calmed a bit at night and let the ocean breeze drop a few degrees. Still, sweat dripped down my spine.

The pendulum stopped.

I froze mid step and stared at the nonmoving blue-violet crystal. *Finally.* I sighed with relief. But when I looked up, all my oxygen left me in a rush. I staggered back a few steps. My body turned cold. "This is not going to go well."

# CHAPTER SEVEN

"You've got to be kidding me." I groaned and pushed my long black hair out of my face. My heart rate began slowing back down, but not fast enough.

In front of me, a brick pathway about eight feet wide stretched farther than I could see. On each side of the walkway were rows and rows of headstones. In the dark, the trees surrounding me were unidentifiable, but I felt their energy calling to me like a whisper in the wind. The moss hanging from the branches swayed in the breeze.

I glared down at the pendulum. "Is this the next location in the prophecy?"

It swung a *yes* so wide I thought perhaps it was mocking me. I cursed. The air around me grew thick and musty, like I'd walked into an old garage. Fog seeped out of the ground and swirled around my legs. A wave of ice cold energy rolled down my spine, making me shiver so hard my teeth clattered. Every muscle in my body tensed as my fighting instinct kicked in. Something inside me screamed to flee and never look back. But I knew better. The guardian spirits meant to keep everyone out, even witches.

"I'm not here to hurt you," I said.

Whispered voices tickled my ears, close but too soft to discern. A flash of purple light made me look to the right and I gasped. Like in my living room when I'd first tried to use the pendulum, the crystal radiated purple mist that glowed like starlight in the dark. It was trying to talk to me. I didn't know how I knew, but I just did. It already told me I had to be here...but why?

*First ally with those between the lands.* That was my clue. I could figure it out. Ally meant be friendly with another group, to work together...with those between the lands. Between the lands? Originally, I'd thought the line referred to demons or evil spirits—*wait*. Spirits are technically between two places, Earth and the afterlife. Evil spirits would never align themselves with witches. But friendly spirits might. They were either supposed to be here, sent by a higher power, or accidentally got trapped here. I looked down at the fog swirling around my feet. The guarding spirits of this cemetery were the ones in the prophecy. That was what the line meant.

I pulled my cell phone out of my pocket and dialed Cassandra. When she answered, I skipped the standard greeting. "The next line means we have to ally with the spirits guarding Holy Grove Cemetery."

There was a beat of silence. "I'll be there in five minutes."

"Hurry." I swallowed down a rush of anxiety. The back of my neck tickled like someone was watching me, but everywhere I looked I found only darkness and fog. I gripped my phone harder. "I have a bad feeling about this."

"Kessler, send backup to Holy Grove Cemetery now. Okay, Tennessee, we're coming."

I frowned. Something in her voice was off. She was short and almost cold. No words of encouragement, no optimism in the face of grave danger. "What's wrong?"

"Nothing," she said too quickly. Her voice was too soft and raspy. It was the tone she used when she was stressed. Or worried.

"Tell me."

Silence hung on the other end of the line for a few long seconds before she cursed. "I figured out the last line."

"And?" I asked through clenched teeth.

"It means..." she said. "I'll tell you when I get there. Focus for now."

"Fine." I didn't push it any further. We were working on the second line of the prophecy. I didn't need to worry about the fourth yet. I hung up the call and slid my phone back into my pocket.

The purple mist swirled brighter around the crystal. I

glanced around me, at the thick layer of fog hovering above the surface all around the cemetery. The mausoleums in the back seemed to be floating on clouds.

I cleared my throat. "Guardian spirits, please show yourselves and talk to me." I waited but nothing happened. Was there some kind of trigger word to get their attention? Communicating with the dead had never been a specialty of mine. *I really need to brush up on my basic magic.*

The pendulum chain warmed between my fingers. I looked down at it and narrowed my eyes. I might've been crazy, but it seemed like the tool wanted to speak with me. *Note to self: ask Henley if her pendulums communicate with her.*

"Okay, pendulum, am I doing this right?"

*No.*

I huffed. "Was I close?"

*NO.*

"Okay...can they hear me?"

*Yes.*

So, they heard me but didn't answer. Interesting. Perhaps it required a certain type of power? "Am I capable of calling upon them?"

*No.*

*Is it possible for a crystal to laugh at me? Because I think so.* I sighed in defeat. "So, I need to wait for Cassandra?"

*Yes.*

I didn't have much time before the others arrived and the pendulum stopped responding to me. There had to be more information it could give me. "Do I need the other Coven Cards here with me tonight, in this cemetery?"

*Yes.*

I cursed. If I needed all of my backup, it wasn't going to be pretty. "Are we about to be attacked?"

*YES.*

Headlights lit up the headstones to my right. A glance over my shoulder told me at least one car of backup had arrived.

I returned my attention to the pendulum. "Cassandra says she knows what the last line of the prophecy means. Is she right?"

*Yes.*

"Is it a task I will have to complete?"

*Yes.*

No time to react to that yet. "Can I bring backup with me to do it?"

*NO.*

My heart sank. *Why me?*

*I don't want to answer.*

I jumped, unaware I'd spoken out loud. Great, another solo quest.

Another set of headlights lit up the gravestones. My time was up.

"Do I need you anymore in this cemetery?"

*No.*

"Tennessee?" Cassandra yelled out from the entrance of the cemetery behind me.

"I'm here."

Without the headlights, the crescent moon barely gave off enough light to see, and the heavy flock of trees blocked most from getting to me. I willed my power to full force and felt it power through my veins like a firehose. Bright white light illuminated everything around me in at least a thirty-foot radius. The pendulum chain turned cool between my fingers, like it had gone to sleep. I carefully tucked it into my front pocket. I had never seen a pendulum that seemed so *alive*.

"Hey, most of us are here. Did you have any luck with the spirits?" Cassandra's voice was still off, and she wouldn't meet my eyes.

"The pendulum says you're right." When she turned wide eyes on me, I held up my palms to stop her. "Whatever theory you came up with about the last line, it's correct. I asked the pendulum. It also confirmed that I'll be the one assigned, and alone. So just tell me."

Her face fell and her shoulders dropped. She nodded. "The vengeful Fallen's call... It means the Gathering."

I threw my head back and cursed louder than I had any right to inside a cemetery. Me, at the Gathering. "Does Kessler know?"

"Yes." She took a deep breath. "I explained it all to him, but for right now, we have to focus on this task."

How was I supposed to focus on this task knowing what task awaited me next? I didn't even understand what I had to do for this one. Join forces with some friendly ghosts, fight some demons, and hope I accomplished the unknown task. Then go to the Gathering, fight some more unfriendlies, and hope I accomplished an even bigger task.

*Sounds like a solid plan.* I sighed and stretched my arms to relieve some stress. I had to trust the Goddess and Cassandra here. Fighting was my specialty. If I focused on that, I might just come out on top. Otherwise, why would She have chosen me for this quest?

"We're about to be attacked." I glanced around at the thickening fog. "The pendulum told me."

# CHAPTER EIGHT

S he didn't freak out, jump, or scream. No, instead she turned her gaze on our surroundings. "Then I better get making allies with the friendlies. Get everyone ready for battle. I'm not sure what we're dealing with, but it won't be our norm."

Cassandra knew what she had to do; she didn't need me hovering over her. Nor would I be any help, as I failed to summon the friendlies a few minutes prior.

I nodded and turned to look for my Coven. In the minute I stopped to talk with Cassandra, the rest of the gang had arrived. They stood just inside the entrance on the brick pathway. Some of them watched Cassandra behind me, some took in my glowing body and tensed, and some had their eyes on the cemetery. But not a single one of them looked scared. Battle was what we did. They were ready.

*I* was ready. This was my zone. After hours of confusion and scratching my head, it felt nice to be comfortable in my skin.

I walked up to the group and met their heavy stares. "Henley, go help Cassandra and watch her back."

"On it." Henley wasted no time in racing to catch up with our fearless priest.

I turned back to the rest. "This isn't going to be a normal fight. We need to break off into teams. Royce, Chutney, and Libby, take the east side. Easton, Lily, and Willow, take the north side. Paulina, Braison, and Larissa, take the south side. Cooper, Peabo, Atley, and Kessler, take the west side. We're going to need magic and a sword."

"Solid combos, boss. Let's do this, ladies!" Easton waved at his two partners and ran off.

Somewhere in the back of my mind, I registered the fact I just gave Kessler an order, but I didn't have time to process it. I held my right hand out and called for my sword. My energy flexed and flashed across my friends' faces. I took one more glance around my crew before turning and heading deeper into the cemetery. My fingers tingled in warning of my incoming weapon. I reached out and let the hilt slam into my palm without slowing my pace.

A whistle cut through the silent night sky. It flared a

brilliant red arc like a comet and slammed into the bricked pathway about twenty feet back. Fragments of concrete and dirt flew in the air. The ground rumbled under my feet. Crimson smoke billowed down the center walkway, swirling and thickening until it began to take form. Streaks of red flashed across the black sky in the distance like shooting stars, moving in sporadic directions.

"Stand your ground," I yelled to everyone. I gripped my weapons and moved closer. Whatever it was, it was going to go through me first.

The red smoke morphed into a wolf the size of a moose. It raised its translucent scarlet nose to the sky and howled. The other streaks in the sky took sharp turns and headed straight toward us. Within seconds, more than a dozen red beams crashed into the cemetery like asteroids. Whatever this thing was, it just called in for backup. Maybe they'd been searching the city looking for us.

I kept my eyes on the massive wolf in front of me, with my weapons ready to fly. The beast howled again, and this time its call was answered. The other wolves stalked through the cemetery to join their friend.

"Hold still," I shouted. We had no idea what these things were yet. We needed to tread carefully. "Do not engage first."

The biggest wolf, the one who'd gotten there first, nodded its big head to the left and then right before returning its transparent gaze on me. It snarled and lowered its head to the ground...and disappeared. The wolves behind it vanished, leaving only the red smoke hovering over the ground.

"What the hell?" Easton yelled from behind me.

"Did they leave?" Larissa asked.

"Hold steady!" I shouted.

This was only the beginning. I flexed my muscles and bounced on the balls of my feet, ready to move. My body tingled with adrenaline and power. The glow off my skin illuminated a good five feet around me.

The red smoke slithered between gravestones, spreading farther across the cemetery. A gust of wind slammed into my face and whipped around my body. It howled like the wolves. Maniacal laughter bubbled up from the ground.

"How we doing over there, George?" I yelled out to Cassandra.

The prophecy had said we needed allies for a reason. I didn't want to start a battle without them.

"Almost!" Cassandra shouted back.

Before I could respond, the ground trembled like an earthquake. Bright red lights blasted out from the ground and lit up the sky. High-pitched shrieks pierced my eardrums, but I held still.

"*Los muertos,*" Paulina shouted from far behind me.

I frowned and opened my mouth to ask what she meant

when the ground in front of me exploded and skeletal hands reached out of the dirt. They clawed and pushed the earth around until an entire human body emerged from the grave. My pulse quickened and my breath hitched. This was something straight out of a horror movie. I watched in terrified silence as dozens of skeletons climbed out of the ground. The red smoke snaked around each figure and filled the empty rib cages. The eye sockets flared to life with little fireballs for eyes. Some of them were missing bones and body parts, but it didn't seem to stop them from stalking toward us.

"They possessed the bones!" Paulina shouted, but I'd already figured that much out.

"Hold your fire!" I ordered. We needed our allies. "Cassandra!"

The second I yelled her name, the skeletons charged. Something glistened in their hands, and it took me a second to recognize it as metal. *How the hell did they get weapons?* My mind spun with confusion, but I forced the thoughts away.

I took a deep breath and eyed my opponent. "Now!" I yelled and sprinted forward.

The battle cries of my Coven sounded behind me, but I didn't look back. I raced straight for the skeleton demons and swung my weapons. The monster's skill was no match to mine. In seconds, I sliced through its spine and sent the bones crumbling to the ground. I grinned and bounced back to destroy another when the pieces began to reassemble. *What the hell?*

I cursed and jumped backward to give myself room. They didn't die. Whatever I chopped off just reattached itself. The skeleton raised its weapon and charged toward me, but before I could react, a wall of glimmering blue jumped in front of me. I gasped and froze mid swing.

The blue figure grabbed the skeleton by the neck and turned to face me. "Now!" it bellowed.

Without hesitating, I let my sword hand fly in a perfect arc, slicing up the middle of the skeleton. The translucent blue figure solidified until I recognized it as a spirit.

*She did it.* I was so excited to see the ghost I almost missed it slam the broken bones of the demon back into the grave.

The spirit turned to me with his hand held out and yelled, "Give me your dagger, soldier!"

I blinked in surprise but handed over my weapon. The spirit grabbed it from my hand and stabbed the demon in the skull. Red light flashed, and then the smoke vanished.

The spirit turned toward me, held his fingers up to his lips, and whistled louder than a freight train. He was dressed like a colonial soldier and held a bayonet in his right hand. A second later, a squadron of transparent, glowing blue spirits appeared behind him, each strapped with a bayonet and a knife.

The spirit holding my dagger turned his gaze to me

and grinned. He actually grinned. "You all take 'em down, and we'll send 'em back. Got it?"

I nodded and snapped my jaw shut. *Ally with those between the lands.* These demons couldn't be killed the normal way. We needed a spirit's help.

I spun on my toes and spotted my Coven battling one skeletal demon after another. "Just slice them down! Our new friends will finish it!"

"General," a whispered voice rumbled close to my ear. "You'll get this back after."

The spirit took off into the battle with my dagger. A skeletal demon popped up out of the ground in front of me and I charged. I only had my sword now, but I wouldn't let that slow me down. Everything around me blurred into a sea of red. I ran, ducked, and jumped over gravestones while slicing my blade into everything in my path. I moved like a tornado, bouncing from one spot to the next without slowing down or looking back. Our allies were trained fallen soldiers. The second bare bones hit the ground, they jumped into action and snuffed out their red smoke.

Neon red lightning flashed through the cemetery off to my left. White swirling magic blasted bones to dust over on my right. I summoned a gust of wind and slammed it into three skeletons chasing down Chutney. Easton's battle laughter echoed off the trees, though I couldn't tell where he was. Two skeletal demons leapt in front of my path with three-foot-long blades. I slid across the dirt and swung my sword into the sky. I rolled and jumped back to my feet. My sword flew back to my palm.

I turned and threw it back into the air like a boomerang. "Down!"

Kessler and Cooper dove to the ground and rolled out of the way. Willow screamed but when I turned, I found her conjuring brick walls in front of her on the fly. Skeletal demons splattered and broke against the surface. I stopped and looked around the cemetery to each of my friends. Their skin was pale and glistening with sweat under the moonlight. I smelled the bitterness of blood in the breeze and cursed. Neither demon nor spirit bled. That meant my Coven was hurting. Libby and Henley's magic were barely illuminating and only traveled a foot or so before fading out. Our allies trampled through, but we were heavily outnumbered. They couldn't snuff out one demon before two more popped up. If only we could get them all down at once.

I turned and spotted Royce slice the head off a skeleton, and an idea came to mind. "Royce!"

Royce's gaze snapped to mine. Blood trickled down his forehead onto his cheekbones. "Why are you still human?" he shouted back like he'd read my damn mind.

I raised my right hand and called for my sword. When the metal hit my palm, I nodded at Royce and prayed he understood what I was about to do. "On five!"

Royce cursed and turned away from me.

*One.* I adjusted my hold on my sword hilt.

In the distance, Royce yelled out to the rest of our Coven.

*Two.* I took a deep breath and willed my power to full strength until my body lit up brighter than the sun.

*Three.* I raised my sword in the air, blade up. My power made the ground beneath me tremble. All of the gravestones within twenty feet of me lifted off the ground and hovered in the air.

*Four.* I looked to Royce and waited. He waved his arms around at someone and shouted. Finally, he turned to face me and nodded.

"FIVE!" I shouted and summoned the heavens above me.

Lightning cracked overhead and struck my weapon. I roared and pushed all of my power into my sword and slammed the blade into the dirt by my feet. White light exploded like a mushroom cloud of an atomic bomb and seared through the cemetery. The second the brightness vanished, I jumped to my feet and plucked my sword from the ground. Bones and skulls littered the ground, but they had already begun to reassemble. Our allied forces let out a wicked battle cry and charged the fallen demons. Red smoke billowed. Shrieks and screams filled the night.

Faster than a snap of the finger, everything went silent. No shrieking, screaming, or maniacal laughter. No scraping of metal blades. No howling winds. The night was still again, like nothing had happened at all. Only the rough, ragged breathing of my Coven reached my ears. Our ghostly allies remained rigid and ready, waiting for a signal to either fight or rest. I, too, hesitated to believe it was over. I glanced around the cemetery one more time but saw only my Coven and our allies. Henley raised her left arm in the sky and stared at the moon. Within seconds, her magic made everything around us glimmer in a soft golden glow, brighter than it had been before the attack.

I straightened out of my crouched position and turned to count each one of my friends. The fifteen of them were bloody, scraped up, and breathing like they'd just swam across the Gulf of Mexico. I wanted to feel excited and relieved since we were alive and on the other side of the second task...but I couldn't shake the tingle of unease in my gut.

"General." A whispered voice rumbled close by.

I spun and found the leader of our allied friendly spirits holding a glistening dagger. My dagger. The one he'd borrowed from me during the fight. He rested the tip of the blade on his empty ghostly palm and knelt before me, and then raised my dagger in the air. His eyes, despite being a translucent blue, were sharp and focused.

I stabbed my sword into the dirt beside me then reached forward and grabbed the dagger hilt with my left hand. A warm shock blasted through my fingers and traveled up my arm. "Thank you."

At first sight, the hilt looked its normal antique silver, but when I raised it closer to my eyes, the glow off my body reflected back at me. The surface was rough and unfinished, but cool and comfortable against my skin like one of our working crystals. Realization dawned on me slower than I wanted to admit. It was black crystal, meant for protection. I held the blade tip up in the air and twisted it around. What used to be a dark silver metal now looked darker than night itself. The black color was rich and had the slightest sheen when moved under the right lighting. I recognized it immediately. Hematite, known for being unyielding in power. My double-edged dagger was now a menace of power and protection.

If my magic hadn't connected with it instantly, I wouldn't have believed it was mine. I lowered my weapon and smiled at the spirit. "Thank you."

He bowed his head. "Now you are ready. Good luck, and goodbye."

"Thanks for your help tonight."

The squadron of friendly spirits stood straight, saluted me, and then disappeared from sight. I sighed and looked back at my dagger. What had they done to it? Why did they do it? How was this supposed to help us? I had so many questions.

"Leadership looks good on you, son." Kessler's deep, familiar voice took the edge off the anxiety rolling through me.

*Leadership?* Heat rushed to my face. I had taken over, hadn't I? It was Kessler's job to be our leader here, not mine. "I'm sorry, I didn't mean—"

"Don't be," he interrupted me with a huge smile. "This is what you do. I wouldn't have wanted anyone else to lead us tonight."

I smiled and nodded. "Thanks." But I didn't feel relieved. If anything, his words made me feel jittery and anxious. Almost claustrophobic. I had no desire to lead, to be in charge. I wasn't responsible enough for the job. How could I keep everyone else under control when I couldn't manage to shower every day? That had to be a prerequisite for leadership. The last time I voiced these concerns to my father or Cassandra, they both insisted I'd grow into it... Except, what if I didn't want to?

"So, who's up for ice cream?" I turned to my left and found Royce leaning against a tree trunk with a wicked grin on his filthy face.

Silence.

Despite the tension coiled in my gut, I laughed. "Rocky road, perhaps?"

"I'd prefer peaches and cream, actually," Easton said under his breath.

The rest of us groaned.

Lily smacked him on the back of the head.

The rest of us laughed.

Easton grinned shamelessly. He winked at his girl-friend, unfazed.

"So, what did they want your dagger for?" Cooper walked up in front of me and held his hand out. "May I see?"

I flipped the dagger in the air and caught it by the blade, letting the hilt be free for my brother to take. "Here. I have no idea why they wanted it, but it definitely got a remix. Cassandra, what can you tell us?"

"Not much," she answered with a sigh.

*What?* From the moment the spirit took my dagger, I thought Cassandra understood why. She'd nodded in approval at the time. All of my confidence left me in a rush, like I'd been sucker punched in the gut. I felt deflated.

"Oh..." I didn't know what to say. She always had answers and explanations. We relied on it. The second I thought that, I regretted it. It wasn't fair to her. I turned to my left, to where she stood between the two trees everyone had joined under.

She ran a hand through her tousled, long red hair. Her eyes seemed locked on something way off in the distance. "Whatever they did to your dagger is the reason we came here tonight. That's why he said 'now you are ready,' but I don't know what that specifically means."

"Why does it look different?" Cooper asked, his pale green eyes focused on the blade.

She shrugged. "Black crystal and hematite. Protection and power. Tennessee has to go to the Gathering, so he'll need both. I had a vision a few minutes ago—"

A dark blade speared through the middle of her stomach. She gasped.

"NO!" Time slowed around me. Everything was a blur of motion and a dull roar in my ears. Blood splashed across my face. My throat and jaw burned like I was screaming, but I didn't know if I was. All of my focus zeroed in on the demon's barbed tentacle impaled through my best friend's body. When my hands gripped onto something sharp and sticky, my brain snapped back into action. I pretended I didn't hear her gasps or see the widening of her eyes with each slide of the tentacle. With both hands, I pushed against the end of the tentacle, trying to prevent it from going any farther.

Screams of rage echoed around me. Bursts of bright whites and neon reds flashed over my head as my Coven's magic attacked.

A shadowy form tackled me like a linebacker and slammed my back into the ground. It pressed into my chest and loomed over me. The demon had glowing red eyes, venom dripping from its mouth, and tentacles slicing through the air. I raised my right hand and called for my sword, but the demon pinned me to the dirt with its tentacles. Lightning and black smoke pummeled into the monster from all sides to no avail. Its beady red eyes narrowed on my face then looked down my body, like a puppy who knew I had a cookie in my pocket.

*My pocket.* It wanted the pendulum. I forgot about my dagger and jammed my hand in my pocket. The crystal warmed between my fingers.

My friends were already tired from one fight, and this demon wasn't slowing down. It wasn't going to stop until it got the pendulum. I clenched my teeth and summoned every ounce of power inside of me until I lit up brighter than the sun. The demon hissed and reared back. There was a pop louder than a gunshot, and the demon exploded like a firework.

I scrambled to my knees and crawled to Cassandra. Her eyes met mine, and everything shattered around me. I yanked my shirt off and pushed it against the gaping hole in her body. The blood pooling under her spread wider and thicker with every second.

"Kessler!" My voice cracked.

"Tennessee..." she whispered. She moved her hands over mine and squeezed. Her skin was ice cold.

"Just hang on!" I begged her. Something wet dripped down my cheeks; might've been blood or it might've been tears. "We'll get help. Kessler!"

"I'm here," my father's voice rumbled in my ear. His hands covered Cassandra's. "I'm right here."

Within seconds, the hands of my Coven, *our* Coven, stacked on top of each other. Energy buzzed and crackled between our arms in little bolts of energy. Warmth radiated from my hands and spread through my body. We were trying to heal her with our magic, our powers. But even though her breathing calmed, her skin drained of its color. Her eyes filled with tears as she looked around at each of us.

"Just hang on," I begged again. "We can heal you."

"You can't," she whispered.

"Don't give up," I yelled. We were witches for Goddess's sake. Surely there had to be something we could do. I ran through my memories of spells and healing magic, trying to think of the answer to cure her.

"Tennessee, you cannot stop this." Her voice was barely more than a whisper. "You know that."

"I don't." My voice cracked. She was right. I couldn't save her.

She coughed up blood and shuddered. "I don't have long now. You all have to listen to me. You remember everything I told you?" Her gaze met Kessler's.

"Yes. I'll tell them." Kessler nodded. "What else?"

She took a few deep breaths. "I need... my...hand...now."

No one moved.

"NOW."

Once her left hand popped free, she wiggled her fingers above the dirt. A rainbow of mist swirled through the air and between her fingers until it formed together and made two rectangles. The shapes dropped to the ground, and Cassandra sagged against the dirt.

I reached forward and plucked two items up...and gasped. Under the bright glow of Henley's intensified moon, two female faces looked up at me.

The one on the left had raven hair, an extravagant crown, and the Roman numeral II etched into the top. The one on the right had hair of sunshine, a flowered diadem, and the Roman numeral III. They looked like every tarot card I'd ever seen while looking nothing similar at the same time.

"The High Priestess and the Empress," I said.

Cassandra nodded and the movement sent her into a coughing fit. "Listen..."

"We're listening," Cooper said softly.

"My Mark will not carry on until they claim their rank. Only then can the locket be found."

"What?" I exhaled and stared down at the tarot cards.

The locket was a gift given to every Hierophant by the Goddess herself. It contained our race's secrets and history all the way back to the fall of Eden when we were created. It was the single most important item our race had. When one Hierophant died, the locket would disappear and wait to be found by the other Cards. And we'd only have three weeks to find it before the locket would return to the Goddess. Forever. I opened my mouth to speak, but no words came out.

"Cassandra...what...what...?" Kessler stuttered and it broke something inside of me. He never was anything but sturdy and strong. "What...does this mean?"

"Find them," she whispered. Her lips were stained red and split. "Find them, induct them, then seek the locket. You must...find...the locket."

"But we need the twins first?" Cooper asked.

She nodded. Her eyelids fluttered and closed.

My heart leapt into my throat. "Don't go."

She cracked the smallest of smiles and opened her eyes. Her gaze traveled around the group one witch at a time, like she wanted to memorize our faces before she passed. Tears fell from the corners of her eyes. Her lips trembled. I gripped her left hand in mine and squeezed her icy fingers. Finally, her eyes met mine, and I fell apart. This time I knew they were tears on my face. Her fingers twitched as she tried to squeeze back, but she had nothing left.

"I must. It's my time. Goodbye, my family. I love you all so much. We will meet again, on the other side. I will be waiting for you." Everyone choked on their whispered goodbyes and love. When I tried to say something, she shook her head. "Tennessee...look at me."

I hadn't even realized I'd turned away. I turned my head to her. I tried to find the right words, but they wouldn't come.

"I had a vision once. I saw you, the night Kessler found

you, near a riverbank." She coughed and blood spilled onto her chin. "Your memories are not lost forever."

"Thank you." It was time to let her go. I had to. I just needed to say the words. She deserved to hear them. "Goodbye, my friend, my sister. I will never forget you."

Her emerald eyes bored into mine. "Just remember, you are so strong, so brave. Hope is not lost." She smiled at me and closed her eyes one last time.

## CHAPTER NINE

Three hours later, I stood beside the ocean. The warm waves rolled over my bare feet. Sand rubbed between my toes with the pulling tide. Out in front of me, the Gulf of Mexico glistened like a crystal under the amber crescent moon. The water was flat and calm. The salty breeze blew my long hair into my face, and it broke off another little piece of my soul. Cassandra had been offering to trim it. She'd said I looked wild with it long and shaggy. She'd wanted to clean me up. Now she'd never get the chance. Something so insignificant shouldn't hurt so much.

But it did. There were so many little things I'd miss about her. Over the next few months, I was bound to say something that'd remind me of her. I'd make our inside jokes only to belatedly realize the other half of the joke was no longer there. And I'd break a little more each time. I didn't know how long it would take to heal, or if I ever would. How many family members could a person lose before they lost themselves?

Someone walked up beside me. Their shoulder brushed against mine. I recognized the scent of his Irish Spring soap. *Cooper.* The chaos roaring inside me calmed a little.

"You still have family," he whispered over the lull of crashing waves. "You hear me?"

I swallowed a lump in my throat and tried to hold myself together. Cooper always had a knack for knowing what I was feeling. My adoptive brother didn't express emotions often or easily, so hearing the words from him was almost too much to bear.

"Tennessee, you hear me?" he said with a little more strength. "You still have us."

I nodded but didn't trust myself to speak.

A warm, large arm wrapped around my back and squeezed my right shoulder. I didn't need to look or ask. I knew who it was. This single, simple gesture had been his signature since the very moment we met. Not many things provided me with more comfort, even if I wasn't great at expressing it to him. I closed my eyes and leaned into Kessler's embrace, just like I had the day he found me. The day we became family.

Kessler cleared his throat. "We're ready when you are, boys. No rush."

I stared at the ocean a few moments longer. How was I going to get through this in one piece? I choked back tears and tried to swallow the ball in my throat.

"Let's give her the farewell she deserves, my brother."

I turned and found Cooper's pale green eyes watching me. He smiled but it was full of sadness. I nodded. Eventually I'd have to speak. I just wasn't ready now. *I can do this. For her.* When I turned, the sight took my breath away. I stopped in my tracks and looked at each of their faces.

Most of our kind chose to live in our sanctuary city of Eden, where they'd be safe from demons, sinister spirits, or any other kind of monster. It was the one piece of holy ground the Goddess provided for her people. There was a school where witches attended to learn normal Sapien things, all magical things, and for the worthy, a warrior training program. Once adults, those warriors would be sent out to guard and protect, much like the Sapien military. Florida had always been a hot spot for demon activity, even back before it had an actual name. As a result, a small community of witches built up in The Sunshine State. There weren't quite as many of us after The Great Loss fifteen years back, but every single witch who survived it was staring back at me now.

I'd never seen a funeral put together quite so fast, and it almost warmed the ice in my heart to see the effort they made for her. Cassandra had always said when she passed, she wanted to sail away on the ocean at midnight, in a bed of flowers and crystals with the moonlight to guide her home. I hoped she somehow knew.

They stood in a semicircle, dressed in a witch's ceremonial white. Those who weren't holding babies held their neighbor's hands. All of their gazes focused on the sand in front of them...where Cassandra lay in a wooden raft. She'd had specific instructions for when she passed, and I was relieved to see everyone had held up their end of the deal. Willow, our gifted conjurer, had summoned a wooden raft that looked a lot like a canoe for Cassandra to take her last ride in. Inside, her body was buried beneath countless flower petals of various colors and shapes. On top of those were precious crystals I knew without asking had been handpicked just for her.

Kessler had his arms wrapped around our shoulders. Which was good since I wasn't sure I'd still be standing without him.

He cleared his throat, and the crowd's attention turned to him. "It's time we say goodbye to our Lady George."

*Lady George.* It was an inside joke and a beloved nickname.

My fellow Cards, who weren't currently holding me upright, stepped forward and formed a tight circle around her raft. They placed their left hands palm-up in their neighbor's right hand. After a second, each open palm held a small flame. Henley whispered a few words, and Cassandra's raft lifted into the air. The circle's magic carried her down the beach, with the crowd right behind them holding candle-less flames of their own.

I stood there numb to my core...just watching. The Mark on her left forearm had faded from black to a soft purple. The lines of prophecy written below had disappeared altogether. I pushed the image out of my mind and let those thoughts drift away. A part of me wanted to join the circle and walk her raft into the ocean. The bigger part of me knew I didn't have the strength. I took solace in knowing Cooper and Kessler stayed beside me, like they, too, couldn't handle it.

Once the circle had walked completely into the ocean, they stepped back and gently lowered her onto the water. The rest of our community put their feet in the waves and sent their flames to the surface. Within seconds, Cassandra's raft floated out to sea surrounded by a circle of loving flames to guide her soul to the other side. We watched in silence until a white glow lit up the sky and pulled her in.

The Goddess had taken her home.

My breath hitched, and I choked on a sob. She was gone. *And it's all my fault.* For years, she'd encouraged me to take the lead, to assume the Emperor's role. She'd said it would be natural for me. She'd said I'd excel and carry the Coven to greatness. I never wanted to. I insisted I wasn't fit for the job. No one believed me then. Maybe they'd believe me now? I'd done it. I'd taken control of the quest and became the leader they wanted me to be. Look where it landed us. I sniffed through the burning in my nose. I should've known better. I should've checked to make sure the cemetery was clear. It was my fault. I wondered if everyone would hate me for it.

I didn't know how long I stood there, staring at the sea without moving or speaking. When I finally broke free of my own torment, I noticed it was only those closest to her left.

"She knew she wasn't going to make it to the end," I heard myself say.

"If so, then she was prepared," Kessler said softly and squeezed my shoulder. "Seek peace in that, if you can."

I nodded. At some point, I knew it would comfort me, but in the moment, it only stung more. I wished she'd told me. I wished I could've prepared myself. I wished... I stopped that train of thought. It wouldn't do me any good. I had a job to do. Now more than ever, I had to follow through.

I cleared my throat. "I leave for Eden in the morning."

# CHAPTER TEN

The door to the private jet opened, revealing a narrow set of steps that dropped down to the tarmac. I sighed and slid my sunglasses into place. My eyes were bloodshot and tired; I didn't need anyone to see that. This quest was more important than anything I'd ever done before. I needed to look confident and strong, even if I was a tangled ball of knots inside.

"Good luck, Tennessee."

I paused on the top step and glanced over my shoulder at Walter, the pilot and owner of the plane. "Thanks, Walt."

"I'll be hanging around until you're ready to go home." He smiled and I tried to absorb some of his happy energy. "I know you'll make Cassandra proud."

*Damn it.* My stomach turned. I forced a smile and

nodded. *Talk about pressure.* Kessler had suggested I wait until the last minute to head up here, to give myself time to recoup, but truth was I didn't have the time. *We* didn't have time. The Gathering was only a matter of hours away, and I still had a lengthy drive through the Smoky Mountains to get there. Besides, this wasn't a loss I would recover from quickly.

*One step at a time.* I took a deep breath and descended the stairs. I had no idea what kind of greeting I'd find when I arrived, but I certainly hadn't expected to be met by the Coven leaders themselves. At least not on the landing strip. Seeing them waiting there for me felt like I was about to be executed.

The entire witch race was led by the Coven of Cards, twenty-two of the most worthy, hand selected by the Goddess. Of the Cards, two were chosen to be our leaders: one male and one female. They were our rulers, our King and Queen so to speak. Timothy Roth and Constance Bell sat in those thrones for the last fifteen years. I'd only seen them a few times in my entire life, and yet there they were.

I stepped up in front of them and paused. What was protocol for greeting them? Did I bow? Shake their hands? I silently chastised myself for not asking Kessler these questions before I left.

"Welcome back to Eden, Tennessee," Constance, the Justice Card, said with a warm smile. She held her left hand out. Shaking with your Marked arm was standard for Cards, so I took it. "I'm Constance."

"Thank you, and yes, I remember you." I smiled, relieved by the casual nature of the greeting. I looked to her left at the big burly man with a thick salt-and-pepper beard and flannel shirt. He didn't look pleased to see me at all, but I held my left hand out for him anyway. "Timothy Roth, right?"

Timothy Roth, the Judgement Card, shook my hand but didn't crack the slightest of smiles. He stood slightly taller than my six foot two, but his shoulders were the same size as mine. I took an odd comfort in this until I met his stare. His eyes were a dark brown and looking at me like I might stab him in the back the second he turned around. Then again, I was the Emperor...the Card who almost *always* sat in a throne. I supposed he had a reason to worry, regardless of how much I didn't want his seat of power.

"Tennessee Wildes, it's been a while," he said.

"Thank you for seeing to me on such short notice."

"By what Kessler said, we don't have much time to get you up on that mountain," Timothy grumbled. He didn't sound happy to be helping me at all. "Though he didn't explain why you *had* to be at the Gathering this year. We usually don't allow Cards to attend. It can be too dangerous for everyone."

Well, at least that explained some of his resentment. I held my hands behind my back to try and appear calm and confident. "I apologize for the lack of communication on our end. The last few days have been a whirlwind. We didn't know I'd be here today until last night. Otherwise we would've made appropriate arrangements ahead of time."

Timothy smirked. "Well mannered, I see."

I smiled and nodded. "Kessler raised me well."

"I will applaud him for it when I get the chance. For now, perhaps you could fill us in?"

I took a deep breath and caught them up to speed on the quest at hand, giving only the necessary details. The pendulum warmed in my front pocket, like it knew I was talking about it, but I didn't offer it up for show-and-tell. Why? I hadn't the slightest clue.

"I had hoped Cassandra would accompany me at least this far, to fill you in on the details I don't yet understand, but..."

Constance reached forward and squeezed my arm. "We are all deeply sorrowed by her passing. I know she was like family to you, and I know firsthand what it's like losing that. We are all in this together, and we will help you in every way we can."

"So, this task can only be completed by you?" Timothy asked, ignoring the chance to show some compassion. "Do you know why?"

I sighed and shook my head. "I wish I did, trust me. I have no interest in facing this alone."

"Timothy, Tennessee will need a car and supplies to get up the mountain..." Constance arched her eyebrow.

He nodded. "Already ready for him. I'll go get it and meet y'all around front." Without another word, he turned and walked off in the opposite direction.

"I'm sorry about him." Constance sighed and shook her head. "You make him nervous."

I frowned. "He has no reason to be concerned," I said, praying she understood my meaning. How many times could one guy say he didn't want to lead? Apparently not enough.

"Perhaps." She cocked her head to the side and smiled. "Walk with me. I have some things you'll need."

I followed her in silence across the tarmac toward a sprawling brick building. Once we got closer, I realized it wasn't an airport but the school. EDENBURG EST. 1693 was carved into the worn-out brick above the double doors. I had always dreamed of what life could've been like if I'd attended school in Edenburg like most other witches. It seemed a cruel form of torture to have to walk through the halls now.

Up ahead, teenagers crowded the hallway. I had no idea what time of day it was, or what the school schedule was at Edenburg, but it must've been lunch or between classes. Students leaned against lockers and goofed off with their friends just like they did in my school. Dozens of voices at full volume crammed into a tight space made it sound like a pack of hungry lions.

I wasn't sure what made them look my way. Maybe it was the heavy echo of my combat boots or the anxiety rolling off of me in waves, but as we walked, every student stopped at stared. Their jaws dropped and eyes widened. Noise cut off completely, like someone hit the mute button on a remote. The path in front of us parted faster and wider than the Red Sea as students leapt out of our way. I frowned and glanced down at my body to make sure I hadn't accidentally palmed my sword or dagger. It had been known to happen to me when I was anxious. But no, my dagger was tucked safely into my left boot and my sword hung from a holster on my right hip. Maybe they didn't see weapons like mine inside the sanctuary city?

I glanced left and right while we passed down the hall. The students whispered to each other behind hands and books. I missed most of what they said, except for one word —*Emperor*. My Card title echoed louder than the *thud* of my boots on tile. Most of the guys looked at me with unabashed terror. Girls, on the other hand, blushed various shades of pink and giggled.

I must've been scowling pretty hard because Constance smacked my arm lightly and whispered, "Don't terrify them." She chuckled and shook her head.

"Why do I terrify them?"

"Because you're the Emperor," she said matter-of-factly, like it cleared up any and all confusion.

I wanted to say it didn't, and that it made no sense at all, except I couldn't. I had the most power, even more than the High Priestess or Empress, and I was made for war. My friends had told me for years that my aura radiated around me like a force field at all times. It simply hadn't been so blatantly obvious back home around *other* Cards. There was a part of me that relished my power and ranking, and it seemed to be growing stronger. Cassandra had spent years insisting I embraced my role... Maybe it was time I started listening.

When we turned left at the end of the hallway, I glanced over my shoulder and found several dozen students standing frozen and watching. I meant to smile or wave, or something to acknowledge their presence, but I was too blown away by their reaction to me.

"Like I said...perhaps." Constance laughed and pulled open a door on my right.

I followed her through a few sets of doors until we reached a lavish office built out of rich mahogany. Constance walked around the back side of a long desk covered in papers and various random objects. She pushed her shirt sleeves up to her elbows and dug through a stack of papers.

My gaze moved to her right arm. Every inch of her skin, from her fingertips all the way up under her sleeve, was covered in an intricate vine tattoo with bright pink roses. Beneath the vine almost looked like lace, or like she had on a mesh shirt. The black ink morphed into a deep red. I gasped and leaned in to get a closer look. It wasn't a tattoo at all; it was a glyph...and not just any glyph. I'd never seen someone with it in real life. All witches knew of it, secretly hoped for it to happen to them.

"You have a Soul Mate," I said.

Constance's head snapped up. Her sky blue eyes met mine and she smiled. A small blush covered her cheeks. "Yes, I do. His name is Daniel. He's the headmaster here at Edenburg."

"Is it true about the crystal heart part?" I blurted before I could stop myself. Nothing like asking your leader a super personal question. "Sorry, I just... I've never met anyone with a Soul Mate."

"Don't be sorry. I remember the first time I met Soul Mates when I was twelve. I actually asked them to take their shirts off and show me." Her smile widened to a full grin that dimpled her porcelain cheeks. She reached up with her left hand and pulled the collar of her blouse to the side to show off the heart-shaped red crystal on her chest. "And yes, the crystal is real. It's where it starts, though it's not as obviously heart-shaped as people think."

I nodded. She was right. When I looked closer, it barely had the dip on the top to make it a heart shape. Apparently when the Soul Mate glyph settled, it crystalized directly above your heart and was always in the red color family. "Aren't there more crystals in the glyph? I thought I heard that before."

She dropped her hand and let her shirt fall back into place. "When Soul Mates have children together, a crystal appears in the glyph to represent them. One per child. I don't have any children, so I only have the one crystal."

"That's...cool." I wanted to ask her more questions about it, simply out of curiosity, but then I spotted a map in her hand and my focus shifted. I frowned. "What is that?"

"The Gathering is a wild party. Parking is difficult to find, and the hike up to the clearing can take hours. Decades ago, the Coven created a parking lot near the top that only a witch would be able to find. Then the hike won't take even an hour, probably less for someone like you. These are the maps you'll need to find them. Daniel drew them for you. He's been there."

I took the maps she held out and scanned over them. "Timothy said Cards aren't usually allowed to attend. Why is that?"

She sighed and rubbed her forehead. "Because we have too much power. In a normal year, the spiritual activity is low, enough to entertain the attendees but not enough to warrant widespread attention or fear. When someone of our standing attends, the activity rises. Nothing too frightening has happened yet...but..."

"But after Salem, we don't like to push it?" I guessed.

"Precisely." She glanced out the window and pointed. "Timothy has your vehicle ready. I've put a charm on the mountain to allow a witch's cell phone to receive reception even if it says it doesn't have any. If you have any troubles at all, please don't hesitate to call."

"Thank you."

"And I know Walter is ready to bring you home whenever you get back, but should you wish to wait until morning, I live right across the street at the house with the big red door. My home is open for my Coven at all times. Honestly, I wish I could go up there with you. So does Timothy."

"I do too. Your hospitality is most appreciated." I smiled and headed for the side door.

"Between you and I?"

I looked over my shoulder. I didn't like the way this sounded. "Yes?"

*"Listen for the vengeful Fallen's call."* She paused, perhaps choosing her words wisely. "The Fallen refers to those slain by our kind. They haven't been seen in a hundred years. I expect that will change tonight. Be prepared for an attack."

## CHAPTER ELEVEN

B*e prepared for an attack.* Constance's words echoed through my mind as I stood between two raging bonfires and thought about the history of the location. If only the tribe who lived in these mountains had the same kind of warning Constance gave me.

In the 1600s, our race's sanctuary city of Eden was located just outside of Salem, Massachusetts. There hadn't been a witch-hunting problem in the new world since they'd arrived, so our people saw no harm in mingling with neighboring human towns...until 1692 when everything went as wrong as possible.

After the original set of witch twins caused the infamous witch trials, our race had to cover it up and relocate Eden. They fled south to the heart of the Smoky Mountains. Unfortunately, the land they chose was inhabited by a tribe of natives and a huge, blood-filled battle followed. The entire tribe was slaughtered. It wasn't a part of our history we were even remotely proud of. In fact, our Coven leaders at the time were so appalled by their own actions, they refused to settle on the land and moved Eden a couple hours away. They put up spells and charms to protect the mountains and that particular piece of land so no humans could ever destroy it. This Gathering party was intentionally allowed to persist as a way to remind witches of our unforgiveable sins.

Every year, on the anniversary of the night the tribe was slayed, their spirits returned to their fallen place. The clearing itself was all that was left of the tribe's land, and nothing grew in it except grass and small wildflowers. Some people claimed the clearing was cursed. I didn't know if I believed it, but standing there, I had to admit I wouldn't be surprised.

No one had seen any of these spirits in almost a hundred years. Sure, minor paranormal activity was reported, but nothing to alert ghost-hunting reality television shows.

*Be prepared for an attack.* Constance was right. I'd been unsure until I set foot in the clearing. I felt it in the eerie chill on my neck and the edge in the breeze. The stars twinkled that telltale golden hue from a black, cloudless sky. The pine trees lined the clearing like skyscrapers, but despite the wind, not a branch swayed. Fog seeped closer to the clearing from between the trees like something out of a horror film. All of this I recognized easier than the back of my hand from my experiences on a nightly basis.

I stared at the crowd around me and wondered if they felt anything different, if any of them *knew* something was about to go down. I'd gotten more comfortable with fighting monsters than cleaning my laundry, but I loathed the waiting. It gave my brain too much time to think.

In the center of the clearing, a collection of snacks and beverages were piled on blankets and left unsupervised. I wasn't sure if the large object in the middle was a keg or a cauldron, although it was probably both. The communal-style snacks between strangers were surprising. Who supplied them? Did everyone just show up with grub like a potluck Thanksgiving dinner?

A ring of bonfires circled around the snack section, crackling and roaring like a pack of lions. Partygoers mingled from fire to fire. Some people wore normal, everyday clothes and held red Solo cups like they were at a regular college frat party. Some guests rocked wizard robes and long lavish cloaks. Women danced around in Renaissance gowns and guys in...well, I had no idea what they called those outfits. I smiled at all the people, both male and female, who rocked flower crowns, had bare feet with toe rings, and wore crystals on every body part they could. Although, when I got home, I would have to ask *someone* why there were people wearing fake furry tails...because that had me stumped.

I tried to ignore the people dressed in all black with pentagram necklaces and acting like this was their territory. Sure, there were the occasional Sapiens who had magical abilities or strong spiritual energies, but they weren't *real* witches. They just tried to look the way Hollywood depicted witches. *Yeah, says the guy wearing all black with a vintage key tied around my neck and a crystal pendulum in my pocket. Did I mention the crystal and hematite dagger in my boot?*

*Focus, Tennessee.* I pushed my long black waves out of my face and tried to rein in my thoughts. The attack was coming...but from where?

I sighed and scrubbed my face with my palms. I'd been so anxious to get here I hadn't tried to pick Constance's brain. *Smooth move.* I considered calling Kessler, but we'd brainstormed all night about it already. I knew everything he knew. Unable to stop myself, I reached into my pocket and pulled out the pendulum. *This is becoming a bad habit.* I'd used Daniel's map to the secret parking lot for witches, but once I'd gotten into the woods, the pendulum showed me the way.

With the gold chain between my fingers, I waited for the crystal to stop moving before I tried communicating. "Can you lead me to the clue?"

Nothing happened. I cursed. Of course nothing

happened. I stood among a hundred people. Although, I wasn't sure if humans counted. Like all the other times I tried to use it around people, the purple mist swirled around the crystal like a snake. Those whispered voices echoed in my ears like a hushed choir.

"Okay, okay. I hear you. Give me a second." I held the stone in front of me while I walked. It seemed rude to shove it back inside in the middle of our conversation. I frowned and eyed the stone. "Maybe I better give you a name if I'm going to keep conversations like this."

The second my black boots hit the dirt between the towering pine trees, the whispers faded and the mist disappeared.

I stopped and raised the stone. "Would you like a name?"

*Yes.*

I grinned. At least the stone liked me. Question was... what name? "Is Crystal a lame name for you?"

*Yes.*

Yeah, too obvious. I could do better. "Rose?"

*No.*

"Violet?"

*NO.*

"Penny?"

*No.*

"Come on, Penny for a pendulum is funny." I sighed. None of those names worked. It needed to have meaning and importance. A name I connected to like I did the stone itself. Cassandra's face popped into my mind against my will, but I smiled through the wave of pain in my chest. "George?"

*YES.*

"Okay, George it is." I grinned and rocked back on my heels. "George, my friend, am I in the right place to find this next clue?"

*No.*

My heart sank. Then I realized my mistake. "George, when I go back in the clearing, will I be in the right place?"

*Yes.*

I rolled my eyes. *Smart ass stone.* "Can you lead me to the clue?"

*No.*

Well I should've known that one. "Will it be obvious?"

*No.*

Of course not. "Are the Fallen spirits going to show up tonight?"

*Yes.*

"Will I need backup?"

*No.*

I wasn't sure if I should've been relieved or not. "Is it going to happen soon?"

*Yes.*

I frowned. "Do you know what I'm looking for, George?"

*YES.*

"But you can't tell me?"

*No.*

"Please?"

*Yes.*

"Really?"

*No.*

I barked a laughed and shook my head. "Am I losing my mind, George?"

*I don't know.*

That made two of us. "I appreciate your honesty, George." I sighed and glanced over my shoulder at the booming party behind me. "George...are there other witches here tonight?"

*Yes.*

"Should I go looking for them?"

*No.*

"Will their presence interfere with my quest?"

*No.*

*Well, that's good news.* "Is there any question I can ask that will actually help me right now?"

*NO.*

*Well, that settles that.* "Thanks, George. We'll talk later." I carefully tucked the crystal back into my front right pocket and chuckled. I'd just had a conversation with a stone. Perhaps I *was* losing my mind, or had already lost it. Maybe I'd spent too much time alone recently. No one needed to know I'd named the pendulum, though. I'd never hear the end of it.

With a shake of my head, I headed back into the clearing. Somehow, if even possible, the party seemed to have grown wilder in the few minutes I was gone. The flames grew taller and brighter. The voices grew louder...and the people at the bonfire directly to my left were now dancing arm in arm around the flaming pit.

The circle's energy called to me. It was pure and innocent, full of happiness and excitement. A feeling I'd never experienced in my life. I walked around the dancing circle, moving in the opposite direction, when my body slammed into something warm. A female voice cursed. I reached forward and caught the girl by the elbows to stop her from falling. Her head snapped up, and our eyes met.

I gasped. My body locked in place. Her eyes were the palest green I'd ever seen in a human being or witch. They looked like the purest of gemstones the earth could make. They looked like peridot, my birthstone. I wanted to lean in close and inspect the tiny flecks of color inside. All of the sounds around me blurred into one distant buzz. Heat rushed through my body and up to my cheeks...and it had nothing to do with the bonfires. My chest ignited, like I'd stepped into the flames. I took a deep breath to rein in my runaway heartbeat. She looked like a wild jungle cat with her dark hair and light eyes. My body went numb, like I was a robot who'd been unplugged from the wall. My heart raced so fast it fluttered like hummingbird wings.

I licked my lips and opened my mouth to speak, but no words came out. I didn't know what to say or do. I didn't know what day it was, why I was standing by a bonfire, or what my name was. My eyes refused to leave hers. I wanted—no, I needed—to memorize her face. I wanted to hear her voice and feel the heat in her skin.

I wanted to know what was happening inside me. "Hi..." I managed to croak out.

Her mouth opened, and I waited on the edge of my seat to hear her speak. "Hi..." Her voice was soft but packed heat I hadn't expected. Like expecting silk and getting luxurious cashmere. It was warm and inviting, luring me in like a siren.

*Say something.*

*Anything.*

*Hi. My name is Tennessee. I love your voice. Your eyes are breathtaking. I'm not usually this creepy...* But none of this came out of my mouth. My lips curved into a crooked smile all on their own. My body seemed to have been hijacked by the jungle cat in front of me. Heat radiated off of her skin through her black hoodie and into my palms still holding her elbows. *Do you feel this too? Tell me I haven't completely lost it.*

She took a step forward, and my hands slid up her biceps. She reached like she wanted to grab onto me. I desperately wanted her to, and the conviction in the need knocked my focus so off-kilter that I didn't see the person approach behind her until they slammed right into her back. She gasped and tumbled to the ground. I reached down and pulled her back to her feet. She smiled brighter than the stars above, and it did something funny to the beat of my heart. I wasn't even sure I was still breathing at that point; the burn in my chest suggested I wasn't. She opened her mouth to speak when a high-pitched shriek tore through the crowd.

The all too familiar sound forced my brain back into the driver's seat. I spun on my toes to face the center of the clearing. My ears rang from the scream, but my senses kicked into overdrive.

*This is it.* I flexed my muscles and rolled to the balls of my feet. Out of the corner of my eye I saw the girl drop to her knees and cover her ears. My body twitched and begged to turn toward her, but I forced myself to ignore it. I was here for a reason.

Bright light flashed and lightning struck the ground three times in a row a few feet in front of me. I took a few steps forward to get a better view of the entire clearing. Lightning bolts hit the dirt one after another without pause, sometimes striking the same spot over and over. We were trapped inside the clearing by Mother Nature's rage. Thick, sizzling bolts of electricity formed a ring, blocking off all escape routes.

The pine trees that circled the clearing were completely blocked off by a fog so thick it looked solid. The trees were swallowed and lost to my sight. The fog shot straight up into the air and connected with the clouds that hadn't been there before. I shifted my weight back and forth between my feet so I'd be ready to move in any direction. The bonfires roared like dragons and blazed brighter and higher until the flames stood taller than the forest around us. The heat off the flames rushed over my body. I soaked in its raw energy and let it fuse with mine.

Shock and terror hit the crowd one by one. Little blue bursts flashed like lights being switched on. I ignored the screams and cries of the people around me. Their panicked energy tickled my spine, but I shoved it away. There wasn't anything I could do for their fear except be ready to fight. If I let my concentration slip, they could get hurt. My power rippled through my body, waiting for me to unleash it.

A wave of ice prickled against my right arm half a second before a man shouted in pain. I turned in time to see his long robe light on fire. He scrambled to get it off but wasn't moving fast enough. Any second, the flames would burn through the material to his skin. I flicked my hand and sent a gust of wind in his direction.

"NO!" A girl's voice sliced through my concentration.

I gasped and spun on my toes, searching for the girl with gemstone eyes. I found her standing in the same spot she'd been in before, her mouth open. But the scream wasn't coming from her. Relief hit me like a Mack truck, crumbling my focus into dust. Her lips moved, but it took me a second to process what she was saying. *Slow down? What does that mean?*

"Hey! Stop!" she yelled and leapt forward. "No!"

I followed her gaze toward the edge of the clearing just as lightning ripped through a woman in a Renaissance dress. Her pained shriek pierced through the haze in my brain, and I snapped to attention. *Damn it, Tennessee.* A person in a black-hooded cloak ran by me in a mad dash for the forest.

"No! Stop!" The girl next to me shouted again.

I aimed my energy at the fleeing form. Lightning struck the ground at the person's feet like a sharpshooter with a split-second delay. Out of the corner of my eye, I saw the girl next to me duck down and cover her eyes, like she didn't want to see someone else get struck. *Not on my watch.* I threw my palms out and pushed a gust of wind at the person's side and sent them crashing to the dirt with a heavy *thud* just as lightning blasted the spot they'd been in. They didn't move even an inch, but my hyper senses caught the beating of their heart.

I exhaled and my breath billowed in front of me like a white cloud. Arctic chills prickled against my exposed skin, but the power racing through my body prevented the cold from hitting me. All around me, puffs of smoke escaped people's mouths as the temperature in the clearing plunged below freezing. Any second, the ground would turn to ice. Fire wasn't my element, I couldn't control it, but I could control the air around it. I held my hands out to the side and drew the fire's energy toward me. With a swirl of my fingers, I pulled out little flames the size of quarters and pushed them through the air to bring the temperature to a safe temperature for summer clothing. I needed them to not get frostbite or hypothermia before I saved their lives.

I took a few steps forward to force the heat through the crowd. The girl with gemstone eyes called out. Her words were drowned by the raging fire until I focused on the sound of her voice.

"Where are you?"

I knew it made no sense for her to be talking to me, but my body turned toward her anyway. My eyes found her in an instant, like they were programmed to her like a GPS. I *knew* she wasn't looking for me, but watching the relief in her face when her tall blonde friend gripped her hand twisted something inside of me.

"What's happening?" the blonde friend cried. Even from ten feet away, I saw the tears pooling in her blue eyes.

"I...I..." the raven-haired beauty stuttered. Her gemstone eyes were clear of tears, but wide enough to see the white all the way around. Her shock dissolved into what I could only assume was concentration. She snapped her head back and forth, like she was looking for an escape. "I don't know!"

But I knew exactly what was happening. The Fallen were preparing to materialize. This was just the pregame. *Damn it, Tennessee. Focus. This is it. This is why you're here.* I didn't know why this stranger had such an effect on me, and I didn't have time to process it. I had a job to do, and if I screwed it up, the whole world would suffer...forever.

We only had one shot to close the Gap.

And we couldn't do it if I failed this quest.

The air sizzled and snapped, a sound only a witch would hear. I unsheathed my sword from my hip holster and rolled to my toes. *Be prepared for an attack? Yeah, I'm ready.*

A loud noise like a freight train rumbled over my head. The bonfires towered into the sky, standing indestructible as sustained wind swept people off their feet and threw them away like tumbleweeds. I tightened my grip on my sword and leaned into the hurricane, my power keeping me upright without any effort. Any second now, the Fallen would show themselves.

A man with a furry tail strapped around his hips dropped to the ground and tried to crawl away, his fingers digging into the dirt. I stepped forward to help him, but a gust of wind got there first. It plucked him off the ground like he weighed no more than a feather and threw him right into the bonfire.

"No!" I sprinted forward, but I was too late. The flames had already claimed him. I cursed and summoned rain from the sky. I used my full strength of power and pulled water from the sky like a tsunami, like I'd busted the dam in the clouds. It was all I could do to combat the flames until the Fallen came out. But the fires blazed on unaffected.

"Come on! Show yourselves!" I shouted. I hated waiting. I loathed the helpless feeling pulling me under like a riptide.

I scanned my surroundings, searching for any sign of the tortured spirits, but all I found was mass panic and chaos. Partygoers latched on to each other to try and anchor themselves against the storm while others fled toward the forest like a wild stampede. The wind held strong, lifting people off the ground and soaring them through the air. I raised my hands and pushed as much power as I could at each person to shove them back to safety.

A bolt of lightning thicker than a tree trunk struck the dirt in front of me. White light flashed, and the earth exploded under impact. People were thrown into the air like volcanic ash. I ducked and dove out of the way, rolling into a somersault before landing back on my feet a few feet away. Shrieks of terror pierced my ears, but before I could turn toward the sound, a surge of wind slammed into the clearing hard enough that even I had to brace myself against its force.

Faster than a blink, every bonfire went out. There wasn't a hint of smoke, like someone had flipped a switch on the flames. *Not someone...the Fallen.*

I stood straight and adjusted my grip on my sword hilt. This was it. The wind died. The fog lifted. The fires... vanished. Even the rain I summoned dried up. Everything was absolutely calm. Complete and utter silence. The quiet in the crowd was suffocating. I sensed their fear and knew they were too spooked to react. Once the firelight was gone, we were drenched in darkness, with only the hint of moonlight behind the receding clouds. I considered letting my power light me up so I could see the attack when it happened, but I knew better. The Sapiens would freak out, and more people would be injured. I'd have to let my other senses take over. *Here we go.*

A yellowish mist crept across the ground and swept over my feet like waves on the beach. The glowing fog crawled up my legs before blasting straight up into the sky.

*This is it.* I tensed my muscles, ready for battle. The pounding of my heart was only to push the adrenaline and power through my system. I was ready. This was what I was born to do. This was why the Goddess chose me as Emperor. I did not fear the Fallen, only failure.

The sound of drums erupted from every direction, like

a marching band surrounded us. Each beat vibrated through the ground and into my bones. A low rumble started and grew louder into a chant until it sounded like we were on the fifty-yard line of a Florida State football game. I knew what happened next; every witch did. It'd been a century since it occurred, but it'd been well documented every time it had. It didn't matter. I was ready.

"Show yourselves," I growled with impatience.

Bright white light flashed from within the forest all around us, casting the pine trees in shadow and inching closer to the clearing. With every step closer, the light intensified. In my peripheral vision, I saw the crowd block their eyes from the glare, but my eyes were used to it. My own power glowed brighter from my body than this. The light shimmered and took form until the clearing was surrounded by the slaughtered tribe. Their translucent ghostly bodies glowed a soft white and almost looked like real, living humans once again.

The stories all said the chief would appear beneath the North Star, dressed in his ceremonial feathers and war paints. I'd made sure to be facing where he was supposed to show himself. I wanted to make my presence known to him.

The spirit rippled with orange mist until his identity took shape. His eyes may have been transparent and made of ether, but the haunted rage boiled within. He glanced around the crowd until his stare found mine.

I grinned. I actually grinned like a madman. I knew it wasn't their fault what had happened to them, but it was my job now to vanquish their spirits back into rest.

The chief stomped his foot. Every spirit turned their livid eyes to me. The fury in their glares could've melted snow on the ground. They'd come for vengeance like the stories all said they would.

"Come and get me," I whispered.

A loud chirping noise ripped through the circle, and the spirits took off. People screamed and dove to the ground. But the Fallen soared over their heads in my direction at the center of the clearing. I let me power fly free, igniting my body with glowing light. The humans would assume it came from the ghosts anyway. I bounced on my toes, gripping my sword and waiting for the right moment to strike. When the spirits were within a few feet, I sliced my sword through the air and threw it like a boomerang, cutting through ghostly guts with precision. I dropped to one knee, palmed the dirt, and sent my power trembling through the earth. Just like I expected, humans dropped to the ground and flattened like pancakes.

I glanced up and met the wide stares of six people on the other side of the clearing. They were the only humans left standing. Their gazes were hard and concerned, maybe a tad afraid...but not shocked. I stood and held my left arm out to the side. All six pairs of eyes latched on to my Mark for a second then returned to my face. When my sword slammed back into my palm, the six of them grinned like the Cheshire cat and sprinted toward me.

Faster than any human could've run, the six skidded to a stop in front of me.

"I knew you'd be here tonight when I saw you at school earlier, Emperor!" the smaller of the girls said with a timid smile.

The male closest to me bowed his head a little. "Emperor, tell us how to help?"

*Emperor. They know what I am.*

The weapons in their hands sparkled under my glowing body. Four males, two females...six witches. They were about my age, probably all students at Edenburg. I was used to leading my fellow Cards, not regular witches. But I knew the humans in attendance needed all the help they could get.

"Split up and spread out. Do not engage the spirits unless they attack you or a human near you. I'll deal with the rest. I need you to help get these humans to safety. Can you do that?"

Without hesitation or further question, they nodded and took off in a mad dash like they, too, had been trained for battle. They must've been part of the warrior class at Edenburg. I made a mental note to reach out to the school after all of this was over and find out who they were. But right now I had a job to do.

When I snapped back to attention, I spotted the chief

standing twenty feet in front of me, right at the edge of the clearing. He cracked a crooked smile and raised his hand. Fog dropped from the sky like a blanket. Maniacal laughter crooned within the mist, and the chanting returned with growing insistence.

*Listen for the vengeful Fallen's call.*

Something was about to happen, and I wasn't exactly sure what. But this was why I was here. The quest called for this. Spirits reformed from within the fog and lashed out at anything nearby. I leapt forward in attack, slicing and cutting my sword through their ghostly forms.

"Don't let go of me," a girl screamed, her voice trembling.

I didn't recognize her voice, but when I followed the sound, I found three girls racing through the crowd. The one who yelled was a stranger, but I immediately recognized the shimmery blonde hair of the tall one beside her. My gaze moved to the third girl, the one in the middle gripping the other's elbows. Her black hood slipped off her head. The dark hair could've been anyone's, but my gut told me it was *her*. She glanced over her right shoulder. Her gemstone pale green eyes sparkled like diamonds in the dark.

Several spirits jumped toward the fleeing girls. I planted my weight and swung my sword like a baseball bat so it would curve and not hit the humans. It spiraled through the air, cutting through the spirits about to attack the girls. A smaller spirit flew out from within the trees and dove down. I frowned. Spirits didn't fly, at least not the ones that used to be human. It looked like the Fallen tribe, but it couldn't have been one. In a flash, it dropped down and grabbed the jungle cat by her black hoodie and lifted her into the air.

## CHAPTER TWELVE

"**N**O!" *Not her!* I yanked my dagger from within my boot and threw it as hard as I could.

The hematite blade shot like an arrow through the black sky. My power made the weapon glow brighter than lightning. My heart climbed up my throat, threatening to jump right out of my body. I wanted to move, to run toward her and peel her from the spirit's ghostly grip...but my body locked in place.

In the time it took me to throw my dagger, her two blonde friends had jumped up and grabbed a hold of her. They clung to her right leg and wiggled their bodies like they were trying to pull her back down. It was a gallant effort, but now all three were dangling above the ground.

"We've got you," the tall friend with short sandy

blonde hair yelled, even though they really didn't *have* her at all.

"Let her go!" the other friend, this one with long golden hair cried up to the spirit.

All of this happened with my dagger soaring through the air. Any second, it would hit. At least I hoped it would. I never missed. *Please don't let this be the time I miss.* I knew I should've followed through and chased them down. Hell, the two human girls didn't have enough power to bring them down *but I did.* So why wasn't I moving? Why didn't my body respond to my order? Adrenaline pumped through my veins, and my fingers trembled. My heart tried to claw out of my chest. *Is this fear?*

"We need!" The spirit cackled. It wiggled its claws, and both blondes dropped to the ground.

*Wait...claws?* I focused on what should've been human hands and instead found claws like a giant eagle. *That is not a spirit.* I cursed. It was a demon in disguise.

My body came alive, snapping to attention. I gritted my teeth and sprinted toward them, racing across the clearing. It seemed like I was stuck in a nightmare. No matter how far or fast I pumped my legs, I felt like I was crawling. I knew I was practically flying. I knew my power better than my own brain. I knew by the glare shining in my eyes, the wind brushing over my face, and the tingle in my toes that Royce would've questioned my humanity had he been there. Still, the world passed by me in a blur. Only the sight of her studded combat boots dangling in the air and the sound of my racing heart registered in my mind.

My dagger slammed into the demon's back like a bolt of lightning. It screeched and exploded into a ball of white light. All around us, the clearing sparkled like a disco ball before the demon disintegrated back to its dimension. The girl dropped from the sky, free falling like a missile toward the ground. I summoned every ounce of power and propelled forward, jumping over her two friends who'd already fallen. I reached out...and caught her body in the cradle of my arms.

I exhaled and relief sucked the blood from my face. I looked down and met her wide, pale green stare. I wasn't sure when her arms wrapped around my neck, but I didn't want her to move. A sharp burn laced through my chest like I'd been holding my breath. I must've looked down to her parted lips because they curved slightly in the corners, and a rich blush filled her cheeks. My breath caught in my throat. She was beautiful. Breathtaking. A gorgeous flare in the middle of madness. In that moment, it all made sense. Every doubt I ever had. I knew why I'd never been interested in any of the girls back home, because they never made me feel...*this*.

I didn't know how long I stood there with her warm body cradled in my arms and her face inches from mine, but when it dawned on me, my face flushed and I lowered my right arm. Her feet dropped to the ground. She gripped the front of my black shirt and hauled herself closer to my chest. All of the air in my lungs evaporated. I gripped her waist for support. I opened my mouth to say something to her, anything, except no words came out.

There was movement behind her. Panicked energy tickled the back of my neck.

"Guys, over here!" the tall blonde friend shouted from behind the beauty in my arms.

The other girl with long blonde hair ran up and grabbed her elbows, yanking her out of my grip. "Let's go!"

One second the jungle cat was pressed against my chest, and the next second a cold draft brushed over me and she was ten feet away. Her friends dragged her by the elbows toward the edge of the clearing. I moved to follow them when a hand gripped my bicep and pulled. I snarled and spun with my fist balled and ready to fight. I raised my left hand and summoned my dagger. It answered without hesitation. The black crystal hit my palm and electricity sparked.

The guy in front of me paled, dropped his hand, and jumped backward. "Whoa, hello. Sorry, Emperor. Sorry, just me. Don't kill me."

The witch from earlier, the one who'd asked how he could help. I sighed and lowered my weapon. "I'm sorry.

It's dangerous to sneak up on me." I flexed my fingers out of the fist. The urge to turn and run after the girl was overwhelming, yet I pushed it back.

"Noted. Definitely noted." He nodded and scratched the back of his short brown hair. I hadn't really paid any attention to what he looked like before, but now I noticed he wasn't much shorter than myself. He seemed to be fit, and the mohawk told me he had quite a bit of confidence. His hazel eyes bounced around the area, cutting back over to me every other second. "Sorry, Emperor."

I cringed. "You don't have to call me that. Please, my name is Tennessee." I held my left hand out for him to shake.

"Honor to meet you, Tennessee. I'm Warner." His voice was strong and steady, but I didn't miss the way his fingers shook. "The spirits have gone, as I'm sure you noticed. Is there anything else we can do to help?"

*They're gone?* I frowned and looked around the clearing for the first time since the spirits arrived. Sure enough, the place was a ghost town, no pun intended. Each of the bonfire pits were nothing but black logs, and the snack section looked like a bomb had gone off. There were no signs of any supernatural activity. The spirits had vanished. No other demons moved where I could see. The moon had brightened, and the stars twinkled against a black sky. Off in the distance, the other five witches patrolled the area like they, too, were surprised the battle ended so fast. Humans still scrambled around, some worse for the wear.

I cleared my throat. "Can you guys escort the humans back to their cars? We need to get them off this mountain by any means necessary. If any of them are rattled by what they saw, call Timothy Roth in Eden and he'll help you out. Tell him I sent you."

"We're on it. Don't worry." Warner nodded and started to back away, but then he paused. "You know, Tennessee... I know you were at Edenburg today, but you should come back by tomorrow. There's a lot of people who'd love to meet you."

I smiled, or at least I hoped it was a smile. There were too many emotions warring inside me. "I'll see what I can do. Thanks again for your help, Warner."

Without another word, I spun back around to look for the jungle cat...but she was gone. Not a single person, human or witch, stood between me and the forest. My heart sank. The whole night had gone to hell. I wasn't supposed to have any help and had wound up with six assistants. I definitely wasn't supposed to devote all of my attention on a girl... I glanced at the spot they'd disappeared through. Maybe if I ran after them now, I could catch up? I was faster. *Damn it, Tennessee.*

I'd come here with one job—find the clue to help close the Gap. *To mend the bond between them all, listen for the vengeful Fallen's call.* Well, I heard their call, and then I watched a demon try to kidnap a human. It wasn't unheard of by any means, though it was strange behavior. I had so many questions, and the only person who had any hope of answering them had died in my arms. I had no clue, no answer to the quest. *Did I really just fail?*

I raised my right hand and called for my sword. I hadn't seen it since I'd thrown it at the spirits attacking the girls, before the demon grabbed her. Two seconds later, my sword hit my open palm, and I sheathed it in its holster. Something cold tingled against my left palm. I froze. I glanced down at my dagger, and it was glistening like glass in the moonlight. The black crystal hilt had a bit of a glow to it, an incandescence it hadn't had when I arrived. *Why did those spirits in the cemetery want my dagger?* They'd taken it and changed it so much it wasn't recognizable by sight.

But why *my* dagger? *Listen for the vengeful Fallen's call. What happened right after their war cry?* I ran through the events in my mind. Right after their call, that demon had jumped out and picked up the girl. Maybe the demon was part of the answer? Maybe I needed a special kind of dagger to kill it, and that was why we needed to ally with those friendly spirits? I cursed. *I need to call Cas— Kessler.*

I frowned and raised the dagger closer to my face. My body's glow had simmered but still gave off enough light to inspect the weapon. I spun it around in my hand, eyeing the black hematite blade. Nothing seemed different from when I arrived. I gripped the blade in my right hand and twirled it around to look at the hilt. Again, no difference in the last— *No, wait.* I willed my body to glow even brighter and held the dagger's hilt up to my eyes.

There in the center of the hilt, embedded within the black crystal, a small stone sparkled like the stars above. It was a rich sky blue, like a perfect cloudless sky during a Florida summer. The edges were raw and unshaped. It was kind of an emerald shape, but not quite. I knew Henley would love to explain exactly what it was.

I had no idea what the little stone meant or how it got stuck into my dagger, but I prayed it was the answer I'd been sent here to get. Otherwise I'd failed by epic proportions. I hung my head and tried to think. There was nothing else that could've possibly been the clue. It had to be the stone. I knew I needed to get home and talk to Kessler and Cooper. Constance had offered me a place to stay for the night, but now I wanted to go home and work on some answers before my Coven leader drilled me.

Without invitation, that girl's face popped into my mind with vivid clarity. Warmth filled my chest and tingled down my arms. *I have to at least look for her once before I go.* I took one last glance around the clearing then dashed into the forest. I had no idea how long it'd been since they'd hightailed it out of here, but I figured I had nothing to lose by taking the route they had. One nice thing about being a witch was the comfort and connection to nature. I didn't need my eyesight to make my way through the trees, or to spot other fleeing humans. No, it all registered like I had a built-in radar system.

I sprinted through the forest with ease, using low branches like monkey bars and jumping over fallen debris. Within minutes, the edge of the forest opened up on the other side of a two-lane road from the witch's private lot. I sighed and stood there for a second. I hadn't found her, or even sensed her in the woods.

A car engine roared to life from the unpaved lot. I frowned and stood up straight. When I'd arrived earlier, there hadn't been any other cars in the lot, so whose little black sedan was that? *Probably Warner.* I stepped out into the street, careful to stay near the edge. If it was Warner, I wanted to be sure to say goodbye. If it wasn't him... Well, I wanted to know who it was. I didn't have time to make out the driver as the car pulled onto the road, but the second the car turned to my right, my gaze landed on a pair of pale, gemstone worthy green eyes.

*HER.* I gasped and moved forward, but the car had already pulled away. The back window rolled down, and the girl stuck her head out, her green eyes glued to mine. Our gazes locked onto each other's until the car disappeared from sight.

I should've called out to her...but what would I have said?

*Wait a second...* She was parked in the witch's lot. I frowned and glanced up to make sure I was right. Yep, in the back of the lot, the gray Hummer Timothy loaned me sat waiting for my return. Excitement ran through me like electricity. My heart fluttered. *She's a witch.* She had to be. According to Constance, only a witch could find that lot. Even if a human had a detailed map, the charms around the lot would hide it in plain sight. But her car had been *inside* the lot. She had to be a witch.

I glanced down at my dagger with its new blue crystal. Part of me knew I needed to get home to Kessler, to have him confirm my hypothesis about the addition to my dagger. But I couldn't. Almost all witches in high school range went to Edenburg. She had to be a student there. Warner had practically begged me to come by anyway, so I had a legitimate excuse. I'd figure out a subtle way to ask around about the girl...

Someone had to know who she was... *Right?*

---

I HOPE you enjoyed meeting Tennessee and his Coven in this prequel story! The first book in the Elemental Magic series, THE LOST WITCH, is releasing late February 2018. If you want to receive an email alert when it's available, CLICK HERE and sign up!

Turn the page to see the cover and read the first chapter of THE LOST WITCH!

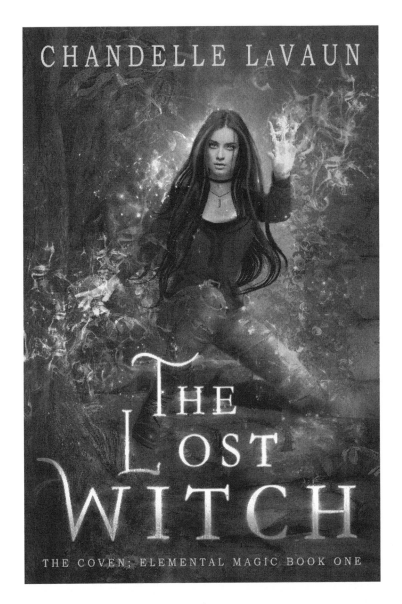

# THE LOST WITCH: CHAPTER ONE

## TEGAN

"Please tell me this is not the spot. Please tell me right now."

I looked up from the paper in my hand. "According to *your* map, this *is* the spot." I threw my hand over my mouth and turned my head, hoping to hide the giggle slipping past my lips. In reality, nothing going on around us was comical.

The air was damp and thick. The night's black sky looked almost gray. Every few seconds, a cold chill trickled down my spine like I was being watched. But when I glanced back, I only saw fog reaching out for me like fingers in the air. Behind me was suffocating blindness. I couldn't even see our car in the parking lot.

"Seriously, you're laughing?" Bettina's voice trembled.

"We can't even see our feet right now, and you think this is funny?"

"I don't have five-foot long legs like you. I can't even see my knees." I turned back and grinned at my best friend, trying to lighten the mood. I didn't want any rain on my parade.

She shook her head, and her short blonde bob swayed wildly around her face. The whites of her eyes all but swallowed her baby blues. "I'm worried about you, Bishop."

*I'm worried about me too.* But it was five minutes into my sixteenth birthday, so I was allowed to be slightly out of my mind. *Right? Right.*

In front of us, across the dirt road, the path was barely visible between the overgrown trees. The entrance looked like a black hole ready to suck me in. I took a shaky breath and tried to prepare myself to go forward. Now that I was here, my courage flickered, but Bettina didn't need to know. I was going no matter how freaked out I felt.

I zipped my favorite black hoodie up all the way to my neck. It might've been a tad warm, but I needed the comfort it gave me.

"It's never this creepy in July," Bettina whined and wrapped her arms around her body.

I grinned. "You think this is creepy, wait till we get there." I'd heard stories about The Gathering since I was a little girl. I'd spent months planning this night... Nothing was going to stop me now. Not even the little voice in my head saying this was a bad idea.

"But I would've thought other people would be here too..." Bettina glanced over her shoulder. "It's only five minutes past midnight. How is there no one else?"

I frowned. No one else? That didn't seem right. Although there wasn't anyone standing around us. I frowned and glanced over my shoulder to the parking lot drenched in fog. I hadn't noticed before. I'd been too excited. *I do now, though.* The night was completely silent. No animal sounds, no car horns in the distance, no echoing voices through the woods.

I cleared my throat. "Hey, Bettina, where'd you say you got this map?"

"My friend who works at the animal shelter with me."

*Your friend.* A lot of random people worked in the shelter. I should've asked this question before we got here. This map might be a fake, or worse, a trap. *No, stop. This is Bettina you're talking about.* My best friend was the most cautious person I'd ever met. She wouldn't have gotten the map from someone she didn't trust. *Paranoia doesn't help anyone.*

"There's got to be more people here, right?" Bettina shuffled from one foot to another.

I took a deep breath to calm my momentary lapse of courage. Adrenaline pumped through my veins like electricity in a power cord. I wasn't used to the rush, but I needed it to make my feet step beyond the road. My ears buzzed. The hair on my arms stood straight up. I felt...alive.

"Let's go find out." I clicked the button on my flashlight, and the beam skittered over the trees in front of me.

*Easy, tiger.* I was amped and anxious, thriving on this unfamiliar sense of energy running through my body. Every inch of my skin tingled with anticipation. Goose bumps spread like wildfire down my arms. I giggled, earning a concerned glare from Bettina who was a six-foot-tall trembling shadow beside me. I winked at my nervous bestie and stepped through the black hole within the designated trees.

I yelled over my shoulder, "Let's roll."

No more stalling. No more overanalyzing. I spun back around...and froze. My breath left me in a rush. *Oh, um, okay. This was to be expected.* I didn't sneak out my bedroom window to back out now. If I just didn't focus on the blackness in front of me, I'd be all right. I loved the night. This was my wheelhouse. Dad had taken me hiking my entire life, including this area of the Smoky Mountains. I had this. My senses were just on overdrive. *One step at a time.*

I shined my flashlight at the ground right at my combat boot-clad feet, then moved it outward to check our path ahead. I glanced over my shoulder and paused. The fog from the road seeped between the trees behind us. *Ignore it.*

I refocused my eyes on Bettina. "Keep an eye out. We've got a horizontal forest out here."

I charged forward, trying to put enough distance between us and the car so Bettina wouldn't want to turn back around. I knew she was terrified. My normally chatty best friend was quiet as a mouse. Even I was having a hard time differentiating the fear from the excitement.

The fog seemed to be getting worse the deeper into the woods we got. If I hadn't brought the flashlights, I wouldn't have been able to see the trees five feet in front of me. Leaves rustled on my left, and I jumped, shining my flashlight toward the noise. Nothing, just darkness. *Probably just a squirrel, Bishop.* The trees had gotten so thick and dense we couldn't walk in a straight line.

*What was that?* Branches cracked off to my right, like something huge and hefty was nearby. I snapped my flashlight over. *I see nothing.* I cursed. The pounding of my heart in my chest thrummed in my ears. *You're in the middle of the woods. Could be anything. Wait, is that supposed to comfort me?*

"Is that a cliff?" Bettina whispered in my ear.

I flinched. *God, I hope Bettina didn't notice.* But why was she whispering? If there was an animal out here, it would've already seen us. Was she trying to freak me out? One of us had to stay strong.

I took a deep breath and shined my light on the object in question. "No, it's just a massive fallen tree we have to climb over. Give me a push?"

Even in the pitch black of the woods, I saw Bettina's face go white. "What! No, you can't leave me!"

"Bettina, you're six feet tall," I said with the calmest voice I had. "You don't need a push. Just help me get up on this, and I'll wait for you."

"Oh," Bettina sighed. Her flashlight wobbled as she shoved it into her waistband. She crouched down and held her palms out for me to step on. "One, two, three..."

I flew into the air like a bottle rocket. My heartrate froze as I completely missed the top of the fallen tree and swan dove right over it. "Whoaaaa!"

"Tegan!"

All of my suppressed fear poured out of me like a broken dam as I dropped face-first into nothingness, screaming like a banshee. I threw my hands out in front of me only a split second before impact. My breath left me in a rush. I grunted and grumbled as my body rolled head over feet and tumbled down a hill. I slammed full speed into a tree.

A deep masculine voice shouted in surprise, followed immediately by several high-pitched screams of terror. Somehow I was airborne again. I flipped and rolled a few more times until I landed face-first on the ground. I spit out grassy hair and mud from my mouth then rolled onto my back. A string of coughs ripped through me while I tried to breathe.

*Well, that was unexpected.*

"Ow!" the male voice yelled again, this time a little farther away from me.

"My bad." I coughed again and pulled more of my own hair out of my mouth. It appeared I'd collided with a living person, or two, and not a tree. "My bad."

"Your bad?" A shrill female voice came from nearby. "You could've killed us!"

"I didn't succeed? Shit." I rolled over to my side and groaned. "My plan was flawless."

There were lots of unfriendly comments after that, from several voices sounding nothing like Bettina and uncomfortably close by. *Bettina!* My heart skipped a beat.

I scrambled to get to my knees to search for my flashlight. "Bettina!"

No answer.

I cursed. "Bettina?" I shouted loud enough to give me a sore throat.

"Tegan?" she yelled back. Her voice sounded way too far away. "I'm up here, on the tree!"

I chuckled, despite the pain shooting through my body as I stood. "You were right. It's a cliff!"

Bettina mumbled something snarky. This, she was right.

"Go to your right," an unknown girl's voice yelled out

from right beside me. "There's a path you can slide down easily on your butt."

"Yeah, listen to the stranger's voice," I shouted. "I repeat, do not go my route!"

The girl beside me laughed. I could barely make out the outline of her face. "Yes, please do not go her route. That one hurt all of us."

"Oh okay, I'm going around," Bettina said. "Who's down there?"

Excellent question. I shrugged in the darkness. "I don't know, but I think I broke some of them."

"Some of us?" another girl snapped.

"I think they're mad, dude," I yelled to my friend.

"You think?" a different unknown girl barked.

I whirled around. "Jeez, how many of you are there?"

"Why, you wanna tally your score?"

"Ow," the guy repeated.

"Oh, feisty. I like it," I said with a grin. Leave it to me to make enemies in a dark forest. "Let me find my flashlight, and I'll apologize appropriately."

"Well, what do you know, someone thought to bring a flashlight," the helpful girl closest to me grumbled.

"You guys didn't bring flashlights?" I asked. When no one answered, I whistled. Aggressive? Perhaps, but I hated when people got mad at me for obvious accidents. "Guess we're even on stupid, avoidable mistakes, then, eh?"

The girl beside me giggled. I narrowed my eyes to try and see her face, but it was no use.

Just then, Bettina's quiet curses rolled into the area. She pointed the flashlight up at her own face and grimaced. "'Hike through the woods at midnight,' they said. 'It'll be fun,' they said."

"Listen, Frodo, you're not the one who just swan dove into a mosh pit of angry humans." I hoisted my friend to her feet. "Now shine your light and help me find mine."

Bettina pointed her flashlight to the ground. I spun in circles until I spotted mine a few feet away. I bounced over and snagged it, clicking it to life as I stood. The group of people I'd collided with froze like deer in headlights.

I arched my eyebrows. "Well, well, well, what do we have here?"

Five people stood in front of me. A tall guy with big biceps and what looked like a nasty gash on his forehead. *God, I hope I didn't do that.* A girl clung to his arm with a snarl on her face and messy brown hair. *Okay, I probably did that.* A taller girl with short black hair and a petite little redhead both had wide eyes and white faces, like they were over the collision and refocused on the dark forest around them. *I definitely understand that.* Then there was a platinum blonde in brown cowgirl boots and a white sweater whose tresses reached her hips. *Interesting hiking attire.* She waved with a nervous smile. *Ah-ha, the friendly one.*

Time to make nice with my bowling pins. I stepped up

to the group and shined my light on all of them. "So you guys going to The Gathering?"

"Yeah, we are." The nice one sagged with relief.

"Speak for yourself. I sure as hell didn't sign up for this," the brunette clinging to the guy said. "I'm outtie. Let's go, babe."

"Yeah, we'll just wait for you in the car," he added. "Don't die."

I cleared my throat. "I'm responsible for that, aren't I?"

"They only came to make out." The nice girl sighed. "You gave them an excuse."

"Okay," I said while trying not to laugh. I shined my light on my best friend. "So...this girl here behind me chewing her fingers off is Bettina."

"Hi," Bettina said quietly.

I turned my light to my own face and smiled what I hoped was a completely normal, sane-person smile. "I'm Tegan."

"Megan?"

"No, Tegan. With a T," I said, still grinning from ear to ear. I couldn't help it.

"I'm Emersyn," the blonde said with a smile and a nervous wave. "This is Tiffany and Mia."

Each of her friends waved when she said their name.

"Well, I hope you're as excited as I am for this." Thunder rolled above us. "We've got a map and flashlights if you'd like to follow us?"

"Thank you. That would be awesome," Emersyn said with a relieved smile.

AFTER TWENTY MINUTES of tripping and fumbling in the dark, I finally saw the hint of an orange glow flickering up ahead. I took a deep breath and inhaled the smell of burning wood. If I concentrated hard enough, there was a low rumble of voices nearby. We had to be getting close. I bit my lip and tried to stay calm. After months of planning and waiting, it was finally within my reach. My whole body tingled and buzzed with wild, anxious energy. After a few more steps, I couldn't take it any longer. I tightened my grip on my flashlight and charged forward in a sprint.

I gracefully glided over broken branches and around bushes until I rounded a huge tree and spotted the actual opening. I slid to a halt. My heart did somersaults in my chest. I leaned against a tree, gasping for air. "I found it."

A few seconds later, Emersyn appeared in my peripheral vision. She exhaled. "Whoa, you found it."

About three feet in front of us was a huge clearing in the woods. From a bird's eye view, it would look like those markings in cornfields people claimed were done by aliens.

"Isn't it incredible?" I asked without looking away.

"Wow," Emersyn whispered. "How did we not hear this from the parking lot?"

"I know, right?"

There had to be at least a hundred people, probably more. Several bonfires burned all at once, flickering across people's faces as they laughed and danced. There were no artificial lights, only the fires and moon above. It was primitive and natural, like stepping into a time machine.

"It's probably late to ask this," Emersyn said with a chuckle. "But what's the story behind this Gathering party?"

"Urban legend says on this night, some unknown tribe was slaughtered in a battle against the witches fleeing the Salem witch trials in 1692. Since then, this land has been cursed." I shrugged. "Most people use it as an excuse to party and tell ghost stories."

"Oh..." Emersyn mumbled.

"I know. Let's get in there," I whispered. I glanced over my shoulder to grin at Emersyn. Just behind her, Bettina and the other girls stepped into the clearing with their jaws dropped.

I took a step forward. Then another, and another. I knew I needed to stop and talk to Bettina to make a plan. To see if she'd calmed down and what she wanted to do... but I couldn't stop my feet from carrying me forward. I was compelled, by what I had no idea. There was some kind of force pulling me in, like an invisible hand reaching out and yanking me in. My body moved on its own volition.

The fog surrounded the clearing like some force field hovering on the edges, waiting for a sacrifice. Lightning cracked across the night sky. Directly above us, the sky twinkled with little diamonds, but over the trees were thick, thunderous clouds. It looked like the fog was seeping upwards and pouring into the sky.

It was creepy as hell, and I absolutely loved it. My attention snapped left to right, right to left as I tried to soak in every detail at once. I felt my lips curl into an involuntary smile. I reached out to my sides and tugged on Bettina's and Emersyn's sleeves. A group of strangers shouted as they passed drinks around and danced in circles.

"Amazing," I mumbled, mesmerized by the firelight.

We'd walked to the center of the clearing in the middle of all the bonfires. A few feet in front of us were large cauldrons that people ran up to and dipped their cups inside. There were people in long robes, cloaks, girls barefoot in maxi dresses with flowers wrapped around their foreheads like vines, and a whole lot of folks dressed in all black. The whole thing felt so...so...fantastical. *Is that even a word?*

"Bettina," I whispered. "Bettina! Oh my God, we made it. We're here. Aren't you happy you came now?"

"Wow," Bettina whispered back.

I took a deep breath as the weight on my chest lifted. Bettina stood beside me with wide eyes, but now they sparkled with interest instead of terror. I knew she'd be okay once we got here. She was fine, except for the mud clumped in her dirty blonde bob.

I spun in a circle, surveying the crowd around us. We couldn't stand here gaping all night. We needed to get in the action. I just wasn't sure where to start. My heart raced and my head felt light and woozy. Maybe I needed to start slow.

I turned back to my little group and smiled. "You guys wanna go over there and join the group by the big bonfire?"

"You mean the one with the crazy people linking arms and dancing around in a circle like lunatics?" Tiffany asked, eyebrows arched as she pointed one French-manicured finger across the clearing. Her red hair looked like fire atop her judgmental head.

"Yeah, and?" I crossed my arms over my chest.

"I don't think so. They look weird." Tiffany wrinkled her nose in distaste.

"Yeah, let's just stay over here with these normal-looking people," Mia said. Her short black hair swayed as she nodded in agreement.

Just like that, the two girls turned and walked back to the bonfire behind them, all without saying any form of good-bye. They didn't even acknowledge Bettina standing in their path. They simply walked around her.

*Manners anyone? I did just lead you here. Unbelievable.*

"Guys, really? Are you kidding me right now?" Emersyn shouted after her friends. She turned back to me.

"Tegan, Bettina, I'm so sorry. I don't know what just happened. I think they're just freaked out."

"Or maybe those people are just weird." Bettina curled her fingers in a quotation gesture.

"You know..." I chuckled, bringing Emersyn's gaze back to me. "If there's anything I've learned from books, it's the normal ones you've gotta keep your eyes on."

"I'm sorry." Emersyn's cheeks flushed bright pink as she stepped away from us.

I shrugged. "It's okay, go ahead. Have fun!"

There was no way in hell I was going to let anyone ruin this night for me. It was my birthday. My sixteenth birthday, and I was at an infamous ghost party in the mountains based on the real Salem witches. This couldn't have been *more* my vibe if I tried. Rain or shine, this parade was marching on in all its glory.

I waved then turned away from Emersyn to let her leave without feeling worse about her crappy friends. I had Bettina. I was set.

Bettina elbowed my softly. "Why aren't we in there dancing?"

I grinned so wide my jaw popped. "Best damn question you've asked all night." I grabbed her arm and pulled her into the ring of people dancing in a circle around the bonfire.

Somewhere around the fifteenth lap, I moved out of the dancing circle and peeled my long hair off my face, but

I still moved in rhythm with the crowd. Bettina's laugh a few feet away made me look over. She was smiling and linking arms with the stranger in front of her. I danced a few more feet out of the way to tie my hair up and slammed into something huge and solid. I cursed and threw my arms out to try and catch my fall when someone gripped my elbows and pulled.

I looked up...and gasped.

If the guy hadn't been holding me up by my elbows, I would've melted into a puddle at his feet. The heat coming off his palms seared through my hoodie into my skin. My knees buckled, but his grip kept me upright. He was tall and lean, with chiseled biceps stretching the sleeves of his black V-neck T-shirt. His hair was black as night, falling in loose waves to his jaw. My fingers itched with the need to push it back out of his face. Tan skin glowed in the firelight like a jar of honey.

When I looked up to meet his eyes, my heart fluttered. He had the most spectacular eyes I'd ever seen. One was a brilliant green, like fresh grass in the spring. The other was a blue only the ocean could mimic. They shimmered like starlight. Goose bumps spread across my skin, and a shiver ran down my spine. My chest was so tight it burned. Was I even breathing? I didn't know. I didn't care.

He licked his lips, and I almost whined out loud, or maybe I did. I wasn't sure. I blinked, completely dazzled. Overwhelmingly so. I struggled to remember my own name. The world around me got a little hazy, my head floating atop my neck like a balloon on a string.

"Hi..." His gravelly voice was low and deep.

It was the most amazing sound I'd ever heard.

I watched his lips, waiting for him to say something else. *Speak, Tegan. He's waiting for you to say something!* "Hi..."

*That wasn't good enough. Communicate. Full sentences!* I licked my lips, then swallowed, trying to relieve the dryness in my mouth. For the first time in my sixteen years of life, I was completely and utterly speechless. *What's happening to me?* I didn't recognize my own body and the way it reacted to him. This kind of thing had never happened before. I stared into his perfect, mismatched eyes, praying he had the answer. Or at least the same confusion.

His lips parted. Maybe he, too, struggled to breathe. His eyes glowed and his gaze stayed latched onto mine like I was a source of energy. Heat swarmed from within my chest. My limbs tingled with awareness. His palms slid from my elbows up the backs of my arms and I shivered.

*What is he doing to me?* I reached forward with my hands to...to...I didn't know what. But I wanted to touch him, to hold on to him. His lips curved, pulling up in one corner as a sideways grin slowly formed. My heart fluttered to a stop, or maybe it was trying to restart?

I took a step forward, wanting to close the distance

between us. The burn searing through my chest suggested I hadn't been breathing. His gaze scanned over my body once, like he needed to make sure I was okay. Heat flushed to my face. My cheeks burned almost as hot as my chest. I smiled up at him. I opened my mouth to say something when an ear-splitting scream ripped through the clearing.

---

I HOPE you enjoyed your sneak peak of THE LOST WITCH! The book releases late February 2018, so remember to CLICK HERE to get an email alert when it comes out!

# ABOUT THE AUTHOR

Chandelle was born and raised in South Florida. She is the ultimate fangirl. Her love of Twilight and The Mortal Instruments inspired her to write her own books. When she's not writing she's on the beach soaking up the sun with a book in her hand. Her favorite things in life are dogs, pizza, slurps, and anything that sparkles. She suffers from wanderlust and hopes to travel to every country in the world on day.

www.ChandelleLaVaun.com

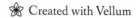

Made in the USA
Columbia, SC
23 July 2021